T0065182

The Spirit of the
NORTH

The Spirit of the NORTH

William Stanley

ARCHWAY
PUBLISHING

Archway Publishing books may be ordered
through booksellers or by contacting:

Archway Publishing
1663 Liberty Drive
Bloomington, IN 47403
www.archwaypublishing.com
844-669-3957

ISBN: 978-1-6657-4867-4 (sc)
ISBN: 978-1-6657-4868-1 (e)

Library of Congress Control Number: 2023915661

Print information available on the last page.

Archway Publishing rev. date: 09/08/2023

DEDICATION

I would like to dedicate this book to my children and their families, whose achievements in life have been many. To Elijah and Charlie, Christopher and Kristin, and my grandsons, Reece and Wesley, I wish a successful and happy future to you all.

PROLOGUE

A blizzard engulfed the cabin, obscuring the building from view. The cabin was a sound structure built of logs. The building stood its ground as nature put on a display of its power, buffeting it with strong winds.

Inside the cozy structure, a fire burned in the woodstove. The family dog lay by the warm fire, while his canine brothers slept outside under the accumulating snow. The trapper, confined to his cabin, thought about having to reset his buried trapline. When the blizzard ended, he would search for his traps and dig them out of the snow.

The adventurers who settled this hostile land did so by choice. A spiritual attachment to nature brought these hardy folks here, who placed their trust in God for their survival. It was a show of faith in a land known as the Yukon.

* * *

The young man and his dog stirred and then awakened when the howl of a wolf pierced the still northern air. The wood in the campfire was burning, as a stiff breeze had relit the smoldering logs and set them ablaze. Johnathan had travelled north to Dawson City. It was 1898, the time of a great migration to the goldfields of the Klondike. Johnathan had struck it rich during the California gold rush and the large sum of money he made from this venture allowed him to continue his adventures as a gold seeker and trapper in the Yukon.

CHAPTER ONE

In the early spring, Johnathan had travelled by steamship from San Francisco, eventually making his way to Dawson on a barge loaded with goods from Vancouver. Such barges delivered supplies to restock what had been depleted during the long winter months in Dawson. They would travel up the Yukon River to Dawson City when water levels were high. This means of transportation was short-lived each spring, as the barges' drafts became higher than the river water surrounding them. A rush to get as many goods as possible to Dawson meant a busy time in and around this growing city once the river opened.

Johnathan had purchased an abandoned trapper's cabin from the Canadian government. He picked up a map at the Northwest Mounted Police office which had recently been built in Dawson. Law enforcement was new to the city, a needed commodity to maintain law and order in a chaotic and dangerous place. The map indicated a route the officers traveled to check on remote cabins once a year. It was not unusual for the Mounties to find the bodies of trappers and their dogs in these structures, typically encountering at least two such deaths per year. Johnathan's new cabin was on the Mountie's route.

The man who had previously owned this cabin had disappeared with his breakfast food sitting on the kitchen table. Cabin fever, a mental illness which gripped men during long periods of isolation, such as the dark cold months of winter, took many good men to their graves. Delirious, these men would run from their cabins into the elements, letting Mother Nature hurry their death. Their madness would end in the deep snow, a burial fit for an old trapper.

Johnathan had thanked the Mounties when he left, with a promise of a visit later in the fall from them. The young man entered the fray of town life, needing to find a good dog, hopefully a Husky bred in the north. A strong dog and a leader would help Johnathan survive in a wilderness unlike California. With no luck in this venture Johnathan had returned to his hotel, where he was surprised to learn from the proprietor a man residing there was selling his dog. He was a fine, strong husky born and bred in Dawson City. Johnathan thanked the proprietor and arranged to meet this man the following day. The dog sounded exactly like the type of animal he was looking for.

The wild drunken banter going on in the streets below kept Johnathan from getting any restful sleep. He was hoping to start his trek to the cabin soon after finding a dog and securing a donkey to pack in his supplies. He hoped to spend one more night at the hotel, and then his wilderness trek into the bush and a new life would begin.

CHAPTER TWO

ohnathan was finally sleeping soundly when a gunshot and yelling from the street below woke him. The young man lay in his bed, eyes open, trying to get the gist of what had just happened. A murmur came from the street where a crowd had gathered, realizing the man was dead. Two anonymous men had settled their gambling dispute on the streets of Dawson and one of them now lay dead with a bullet in his skull, never able to gamble again.

Johnathan dressed and went downstairs for breakfast. The smell of pork frying on the large iron stove overwhelmed his senses as he entered the dining room. Johnathan enjoyed a hearty breakfast of eggs, pork, potatoes and fresh baked bread. The proprietor's wife served as the head cook and baker of this family run hotel. Johnathan was finishing his breakfast when he saw a man and his dog standing by the front desk. He approached the stranger, introducing himself.

After a strong handshake, the man said his name was Jerimiah and the dog's name was Chase. He told Johnathan he had spent the winter in the bush and if it were not for his dog, his death would have been imminent more than a few times. Jerimiah was headed back to San Francisco, to his wife and child, and wanted to leave Chase here in the Yukon where he belonged. His quest for riches had proven fruitless; his spirit and pocketbook were broke. Johnathan promised to take good care of Chase and at that moment became his new owner. The pair hit it off instantly, a strong bond between the two new friends developed immediately.

The next stop for Johnathan was the livery stable, a busy establishment in the springtime in Dawson City. A lone pack animal stood eating hay in the corner, a donkey now for sale. His previous owner was the man who had been shot in the street below Johnathan's hotel room. A deal was struck, and the donkey became part of Johnathan's entourage. Johnathan decided to call his new pack animal Honey, because of her gender and sweet disposition. Honey graciously accepted her new job, happy to belong to someone who would take care of her.

The trio headed to the Yukon River to pick up supplies Johnathan had purchased earlier, items difficult to find in Dawson. The trio reached the docks, where Johnathan loaded the supplies on Honey, who responded with no complaints as to the weight on her back. The small group headed out of Dawson for a new destination in life. They stopped by the Northwest Mounted Police office to report their leaving town. The Mounties wished them luck and told Johnathan they would visit him at his cabin once the snow arrived and the dog sleds were operational. With those parting words from the Mounties, the trio left Dawson, making their way forward into the bush hoping for luck and success to lead their way.

CHAPTER THREE

The trail into the bush from Dawson was well travelled. Like a magnet it drew men into its realm, the search for gold and fur overwhelming common sense, often ending in death and despair for many of these adventurous souls. Johnathan and his newly acquired "family" which accompanied him were now deep in the forest. The silence in the bush was offset only by the hoofbeats of Honey as she walked the uneven, rocky trail. Johnathan surmised his destination was a three-day journey from the city. He hoped the cabin he was travelling to was sound and habitable and its outbuilding for the livestock would be found still standing.

The afternoon sun was waning as dusk approached. Johnathan thought about finding a campsite for the night. He moved his entourage into the forest, finding a clearing which would suffice for the evening camp. He tethered Honey and then gathered wood for his fire. Johnathan would use the campfire for cooking and warmth. The spring days in the Yukon were warm, followed by cold nights. Keeping the fire burning and sleeping close by assured warm passage through the cold night.

Johnathan and Chase enjoyed sitting around the fire, the crackling of the burning wood was the only sound to be heard in the silence of the forest. What seemed like a million stars shone down upon their camp. A sudden howl from a wolf pack broke the serenity of the moment. The wolves were close by, Honey's scent being the attractant. The donkey shuffled uncomfortably, the odor of the predators in her nose. This aroma struck terror in Honey's heart. Johnathan moved the donkey closer to the campfire, where it would be easier to protect her if attacked. He checked his rifle to be sure it was ready for use. Johnathan waited, knowing the hungry wolf pack would visit his camp tonight.

An uneasy silence followed. Johnathan and Chase sensed eyes watching them from the darkness of the forest. The sound of snapping twigs caught their attention, as the wolf pack moved closer to their camp. Johnathan decided to be proactive and stay one step ahead of the wolves. He shot his rifle into the bush; a half dozen rounds in a circle around his camp. He hoped this action would thwart off an attack, scaring the wolves into a hasty retreat. The six rounds led to a swift departure and resulted in one dead wolf which Chase discovered in the morning. A lucky shot by Johnathan had hit its mark in the darkness.

The trio managed to finally get the rest needed for their travels the following day. The sun shone brightly as it rose above the horizon, causing a red morning sky to appear. The morning air was crisp as Johnathan broke camp. He ate smoked jerky for breakfast and fed Chase a preserved dog food he had purchased. Johnathan would do what he could to feed himself and Chase until a supply of fresh meat could be procured and smoked at their cabin. With Johnathan in front guiding Honey, the trio broke camp and continued their journey to the cabin and their new life.

CHAPTER FOUR

The day had turned overcast and cold, a north wind blew across Johnathan's face numbing his cheeks and nose. Snow flurries filled the air, as a late spring storm had enveloped the area they were traversing. Johnathan studied the map the Mounties had given him before he left Dawson. A fur trapper's cabin lay two hours in front of him. His plan was to travel to the trapper's cabin and ask for shelter from the storm. This was not an unusual weather event for the Yukon during the months before summer.

Johnathan led Honey, with Chase taking the lead on the trail. Snow began to accumulate on the ground, casting a white blanket over the land not seen since winter. After a long trek through intermittent snowfall, the trapper's cabin came into view. A pillar of smoke wafted from the cabin's chimney, curling skyward. Johnathan approached the cabin and yelled out, revealing his presence to the trapper inside. The man's dogs tethered outside let their presence be known to Chase, barking and snarling at what these animals perceived as an intrusion on their territory.

The trapper opened his door cautiously, gun in hand. He looked at Johnathan and his group and sensed no threat.

He opened his door to Johnathan, offering him shelter and an overnight stay. The trapper was happy for the company. Only on his twice-yearly trips to Dawson did old Joe, the trapper, interact with other humans. He welcomed Johnathan and Chase into his cabin. Honey found a place with Joe's donkey in a secure outbuilding at the back of the property, near where old Joe kept his dogs. The huskies were the trapper's security system, alerting him to any danger approaching the cabin or the building his pack animal was kept in.

After showing Johnathan his property, the men retired into the trapper's cabin accompanied by Chase. A rush of warm air greeted Johnathan upon entering through the door. A woodstove, carried here by dogsled from Dawson forty years ago, graced the corner of the room. A large pot of food simmered on the stove top. It was old Joe's favorite meal, beaver stew full of nature's bounty of plants from the surrounding forest.

Over dinner, Joe told Johnathan he had lived here and trapped the surrounding area since the delivery of his woodstove forty years ago. The trapper had outlived three of his dogs he had kept as personal pets. He no longer kept dogs as companions, preferring to use them only as work dogs. As evening fell, the storm had passed, leaving a moonlit night which illuminated the white-covered forest. The clock was striking midnight as the men ended their conversation and retired to bed.

The stillness of the night was interrupted by a hungry fox looking for leftovers outside the cabin. These remains were left by the trapper after harvesting animals for food or their fur. Johnathan slept well this night, with Chase snuggled up beside him. The warmth of the fire was a luxury he would miss until his own cabin was refurbished. It would be two more days of travel before his group would arrive at their new home, an ending to this trip Johnathan was looking forward to.

CHAPTER FIVE

The early morning sun shone through the dirty cabin windows; old Joe had not washed his windows since he had received his woodstove forty years ago. The cold front had moved on, leaving the warm sunshine to melt the accumulated snow. Water was dripping off the eaves of the cabin, promising a warmer day to come.

Johnathan ate a quick breakfast with the trapper and thanked the kind man for his hospitality, promising he would return to visit. Johnathan loaded his pack animal, and the trio were on their way. The terrain they would traverse today would be rocky, but forested. Johnathan would watch for small mammals, such as rabbits or squirrels, to hunt today. A generous serving of fresh meat for dinner would be a treat for this group.

By lunchtime, the party found themselves atop a small ridge. While eating some smoked fish the trapper had given him, Johnathan gazed out over the valley below. He then saw movement among a thin strand of trees, a young deer eating grass growing between the rocks which lay scattered over the ground. Johnathan watched the animal, which was unaware of his presence. He reached for his rifle, quietly aiming the gun at the deer. A shot rang out and the deer stumbled and fell dead on the ground.

Johnathan spent the next two hours harvesting the fresh meat. He would take as much venison as he could carry and leave the rest for the predators and scavengers who lived in the forest. Taking from nature also means giving back if the opportunity arises. Johnathan planned to make camp early, as he wanted to cook the meat he had harvested from the deer. The weather in the Yukon was still far from warm, which helped the meat stay fresh for a while.

After travelling for one more hour, Johnathan found a place to camp with a large, fast-moving creek for fresh water. There was also an abundance of firewood in the area, which was good for his cooking ambitions. The gurgling stream provided the perfect backdrop for Honey, who was a happy donkey as she grazed on prime grass. Soon the hot coals of the fire sent the aroma of the cooking meat into the forest. Johnathan knew this smell could attract unwanted predators to his camp, but this time he was lucky, as only an errant fox was nearby to catch the scent.

Chase and Johnathan ate their fill of fresh deer meat for dinner, accompanied by a can of beans Johnathan had been saving for such an occasion. The sound of splashing coming from the creek caught Johnathan's attention. He was thrilled to see trout filling the stream, another food source for this perpetually hungry man and his dog. After dinner, he took fishing line he had packed with him and with found bait of grubs and worms, went fishing. Soon four large rainbow trout were lying on the bank of the freshwater stream.

Johnathan would filet and cook the fish before going to bed, knowing today had provided an unusual bounty of food. Such events were rare in such a difficult place to survive, the Canadian north.

CHAPTER SIX

A crimson red sky greeted Johnathan upon wakening, usually indicative of a change in the weather. An old wives' tale said after this type of sunrise, pleasant sunny weather would be followed by cloud and rain. Johnathan prepared for his day, expecting to see the clear skies change to cloudy later in the afternoon. He would spend one more night in the bush before arriving at his cabin tomorrow. The small party would trudge on, each step getting them closer to their goal. Johnathan hoped to find the cabin still standing and habitable; tomorrow would answer that question.

After breaking camp, the morning on the trail went by quickly. The party came upon a beautiful lake, the water seeming to stretch for miles surrounded by a pristine wilderness of trees set in a rocky terrain. Johnathan and his entourage stopped for lunch here, enjoying nature's glory while he and Chase shared the trout he had caught and cooked the preceding night. After a peaceful lunch, the group of travellers moved on.

The afternoon, like the morning, was uneventful and soon Johnathan was facing a waning sun and a sunset darkened by heavy cloud cover. He decided to make camp under an outcropping of rock, expecting it to rain later in the evening. He tethered Honey to a tree which graced the front of the outcropping. Johnathan then gathered wood from a nearby deadfall of trees and built a campfire. He knew the night air would be cold, attesting to the strength of a north wind blowing.

Johnathan's night was cold but dry, as the dark clouds which had dominated the skies earlier had produced no rain that evening. The morning brought sunshine and a shifting wind from the north to the south. A warm wind would raise the temperature quickly to a more comfortable level. Johnathan's party left early, expecting to arrive at his cabin after lunch. Soon after breaking camp, Johnathan came upon a green pasture which provided excellent feed for Honey. He had not fed her the night before, so they stopped to let the donkey get her fill before continuing their journey.

Without warning, a figure appeared in front of them on the trail. The man, a native of the Yukon, reached out his hand in greeting. Johnathan reached out and a warm handshake was exchanged between the two men. The man's English was understandable, as he had lived in Dawson for two years working as a fishing and hunting guide in the tourist trade, a growing business in the Yukon. Guides and their dogsleds became a common site in and around Dawson City in the early 20th century.

The stranger told Johnathan he was on a scouting trip, looking for wild game as there was not any to be found in the area where he lived. After a brief visit, the visitor disappeared, leaving Johnathan, Chase and Honey alone once again. The man told Johnathan the cabin he was looking for was a short distance ahead. Anticipating arriving at the cabin soon, Johnathan wondered if his expectations would be met or if disappointment would prevail? His first look at the cabin would tell it all.

CHAPTER SEVEN

The cabin shone like a gem at the bottom of a fast-moving stream, a rare beacon of light in the northern wilderness which surrounded it. Chase, excited their journey was over, ran to the cabin investigating the different scents surrounding the structure. Johnathan approached his new home, surprised at the good condition the previous owner had kept the property in. Chase was busy marking his boundaries around the cabin, knowing he would protect his new home to the best of his abilities.

The property had a second building which stood beside the cabin, an enclosed structure set up for the fur trapper. The last owner was meticulous about his trade, the traps and equipment left behind were like new. The inside of this building was clean and orderly, a gift Johnathan had not expected. He would trap fur this winter if someone would teach him how to run a trapline. That wish would be granted once the winter snow covered the land. A sled stood silent in the fur shed, along with a harness waiting to be used by an ambitious Chase. Johnathan's Siberian husky had been born and bred in the north and was an excellent sled dog.

The young man entered his new home. The interior of the cabin was clean and orderly, like the outside of the building. Johnathan surmised the windows had been replaced ten years ago. There was a shed with an ample supply of wood through a connecting door from the main building. An old woodstove, which had seen better days, stood in the main cabin. The stove pipes were in rough shape and created a fire hazard, needing to be changed as soon as possible. Once the winter snow arrived, Johnathan would use his sled, pulled by Chase, to pick up these supplies. It would be a long day on the sled to Dawson, but a doable feat in good weather.

Further inspection of the main cabin revealed a separate bedroom, a table and chairs, and a cupboard for food storage. On the wall was a map indicating the location and route of the previous owner's trapline. This was posted to provide searchers a place to look for the trapper's body in the event he was missing, and someone was sent to look for him.

Johnathan took Chase and exited the cabin. An overgrown path led to a lake, its pristine waters glistening in the afternoon sun. A birch bark canoe, crafted by the local natives, lay sheltered under a thick stand of aspen trees nearby. Another path led to an underground spring, bubbling an endless supply of fresh water from its source to the surface.

The outcome of Johnathan's purchase of this cabin could not have worked out better. The tragic and sudden death of the previous owner was a windfall for his survival here in the bush, a challenge few men could win. Many newcomers to this rugged place perish in a land they do not understand, their existence becoming only a memory after their first winter. Survival here can seem like an unwinnable battle against the cruelties of nature.

CHAPTER EIGHT

The air outside had turned chilly as a cold front approached from the north, so Johnathan lit a fire in the woodstove. After a brief time, heat radiating from the hot metal of the stove sent a warmth throughout the structure, making it more comfortable for Johnathan. After finishing his tasks with the woodstove, Johnathan took Chase outside with him.

Honey was in an outbuilding which had been built specifically for animals like her and Johnathan wanted to check on her. Luckily, a pile of hay lay in the corner of her dwelling, a short distance from Honey's stall. Johnathan fed his hungry donkey and gave her some fresh water from the spring he had discovered near the lake. A secure door on Honey's building would keep her safe from predators, such as bears and wolves. Honey would have to be taken back to Dawson and boarded for the winter. Lack of food and the harsh conditions in the bush would end in death if she were to spend the winter at the cabin. Johnathan had already found her a good location in town to winter over.

The duo left Honey and returned outside. Smoke curled upward from the chimney of the cabin, its wispy appearance disappearing into the sky above. Johnathan returned to his cabin to prepare dinner. He had shot a grouse earlier who had wandered into the front yard sensing no danger. The bird had been an easy target and would make a delicious meal for dinner. Chase lay comfortably by the woodstove, enjoying the warmth radiating from it. He would have many peaceful nights in this spot he had carved out for himself in Johnathan's cabin. Chase was in his element and was a happy dog.

Nightfall descended upon the cabin and the forest grew quiet. The oil lamps had been left where the trapper had placed them, along with a generous supply of fuel in the woodshed, a huge asset for Johnathan. In the cabin Johnathan found a collection of books on survival in the wilderness and short stories about adventures in the north. He read one of these before trying to go to sleep.

Chase was sleeping by the woodstove, lying comfortably on his blanket, as Johnathan drifted off to sleep in the bed. Suddenly a loud crash brought both dog and man back to their senses. A brisk wind had begun blowing outside. Johnathan dressed and retrieved his gun. He opened the door of the cabin, the light from a lamp illuminating his way. Johnathan sensed no immediate danger, and his perceptions were right. When he approached Honey's enclave, he noticed a large tree branch had broken from the tree above. It had crashed down, nearly hitting the roof of her enclosure.

After checking for damage and trying to soothe the frayed nerves of his donkey, Johnathan returned to the cabin, satisfied he had solved the problem. Falling back asleep, the night passed peacefully. Johnathan's dream of a life in the wilderness was coming true. Finding the cabin intact, with all the needed supplies, was perhaps his destiny and a true gift from God.

CHAPTER NINE

The howl of the wolf pack pierced the still northern air. The young wolf pups, safe in their den, snuggled against their mother, feeding from her swollen breasts. These voices in the wilderness were a call to the wild, where both man and beast struggle to survive in this unforgiving land.

The rising sun loomed large in the early morning sky. Johnathan woke from his restless sleep, listening to Chase snoring. His dog was still sleeping peacefully by the woodstove, his favorite spot to lay while in the cabin. Johnathan removed himself from bed; Chase hearing his master awake stood to follow him. Johnathan's plan was to take Chase and head to the lake. The duo would finish watching the sunrise as it came up over the treeline at the farthest end of the lake, a beautiful sight in the early morning sky.

Chase bounded ahead on the path leading to the water. A sudden barking caught Johnathan's attention. As he approached the water, he was greeted by a familiar smell. Chase had surprised a skunk at the water's edge. Startled and fearing for its life, the skunk sprayed its unpleasant scent. The premature reaction of the skunk resulted in

Chase missing a direct hit, a stoke of good luck. He did not end up smelling so badly Johnathan would not allow him back into the cabin. After his terrifying encounter with the dog, the skunk went on its way, glad to get to the safety of his home in a hollow tree on the forest floor.

Johnathan and Chase sat on the shore of the lake sharing this moment together. Canadian geese had returned from their long journey north to spend the summer on the lake. Their babies would soon appear on the water as small dots beside their larger parents, a tempting meal for large pike living in the water or raptors who ruled the sky. Johnathan pulled the canoe from its resting place and floated it in the lake. To his surprise the canoe did not leak, a testament to the craftsmanship of the native who built this canoe. Johnathan put it back onshore, looking forward to taking it out on the lake.

The man and his dog returned to the cabin to eat breakfast. Afterwards, Johnathan planned to take Chase on a fact-finding trip, following the trapper's fur route through the dense northern forest surrounding his cabin. A well-marked trail, trodden down by his dogsled, would make the trapper's route easy to follow. Johnathan decided to pack some supplies on Honey and make it an overnight adventure. He would hunt for meat before hunger took over his and his dog's protein deprived souls.

Johnathan peered out his cabin window. Two weeks ago, the large deciduous trees were bare and the vegetation brown. Now the landscape was green and full of life. It was as if nature awakened a sleeping giant, a miracle only God could understand.

CHAPTER TEN

After breakfast Johnathan gathered supplies for their overnight trip into the forest. He retrieved Honey from her stall and loaded the needed supplies on her back. The trail into the bush started at the fur shed, the building where the trapper's day began and ended. Johnathan led Honey from the cabin to a nearby meadow lush with green grass. He let his donkey eat her fill before continuing their journey. The growing season in the far north is short, resulting in rapid growth of the trees and vegetation. It is a cycle in overdrive, rushing to guarantee life for the following spring. Honey ate her fill of sweet clover and with her stomach full, she was ready to start her day.

The trapper's trail was well marked. When he purchased the property and obtained a fur trapping license, Johnathan had been told the previous owner's trapline ran for roughly four miles. The trails included stops at three beaver ponds. all with a heathy population of beaver. The trio kept a steady pace as they traveled through the forest. Chase would often run ahead, barking to let any wildlife in front of them know the entourage was on their way.

After a two-hour walk, they reached the first of two

emergency shelters the trapper had built along his trapline. These structures were small, having been built for use when the man was unable to get home because of a storm or equipment breakdown on his dogsled. A fireplace, a bed, and a small table were the only contents of this small cabin-like structure. It appeared to Johnathan this makeshift structure would serve its purpose well in an emergency.

The trio continued onward through the forest; their destination was the second emergency cabin the trapper had built. Two hours later, the group arrived at the shelter. Johnathan planned on tethering Honey here while he took Chase and went hunting. As it was early afternoon, there was plenty of time to allow Johnathan to shoot some wild game for dinner. He unloaded his supplies from Honey's back and secured her to a tree close to the shelter. He checked his rifle, one of two he carried with him. Johnathan had two firearms, one for small game, such as rabbits or birds, and one for larger prey, like moose or deer. He took the small game rifle today, as he had no way of storing fresh meat for an extended period. What he shot and killed needed to be cooked the same day.

Johnathan directed his attention at a stand of birch and aspen trees. He knew Yukon partridge and other game birds frequented these habitats. Chase was a trained hunting dog, a good listener who obeyed Johnathan's commands. Chase flushed the birds out from their cover, into the open air. Johnathan shot two large male birds which fell to their deaths after taking buckshot from the hunter's gun. One rabbit was added to their bounty of food before they returned to the shelter. Dinner tonight would be a godsend for this hungry man and his dog. It would also be an invitation for an unwelcome guest, who was hungry and wishing to eat, creating an encounter Johnathan hoped would only happen once in his life.

CHAPTER ELEVEN

Johnathan and Chase returned to the shelter with their dinner in hand. Honey was glad to see them return, as she did not like to be left alone in the forest. Without Johnathan's protection she could easily end up being dinner for a bear or a wolf pack, as donkey was a favorite food choice for these predators.

Johnathan cleaned the wild game he shot and placed their remains deep in the forest away from the shelter. He would build an outdoor fire to cook the rabbit and game birds using some of the ample supply of firewood piled beside the structure's wall. Before beginning dinner, Johnathan took Chase and travelled the short distance to the end of the trapper's fur route, which terminated at the last beaver pond. Recent activity on the dam and the size of the barrier wall which held back the water led Johnathan to believe many beavers lived here. This pond would prove to be his most productive for catching these mammals this winter.

Returning to the emergency shelter, Johnathan built a fire. Soon the roaring flames would create coals hot enough to cook his rabbit and game birds. The sun was starting to set when Johnathan began cooking dinner. The smell of the roasting meat drifted through the forest, attracting an unwanted guest. A large black bear approached Johnathan's camp, following his nose to the source of the delicious aroma of food. Chase caught the scent of the bear and with a low growl gave a warning, making Johnathan reach for his rifle.

The bear also caught the scent of the dog and the donkey, as he advanced closer. Without warning Chase started barking furiously, as the bear sauntered out into an open space, unaware of the danger he was in. Johnathan made the choice to not kill the bear, but to shoot over its head to scare it away. However, this plan did not work as expected. When he discharged his rifle, the bear got confused and ran right through Johnathan's camp, knocking over the cooking food on the campfire in his harried bid to escape. This was a close call with a dangerous animal, which Johnathan hoped would never be repeated during his lifetime.

After calming down from the unwanted excitement, Johnathan finished cooking dinner. The dog enjoyed the rabbit while Johnathan ate the two birds he had shot. The night was dark as the storm clouds moved in. Flashes of lighting illuminated the darkness of the forest. Safe in their shelter, man and dog waited for the storm to pass. Outside, Honey was wet but safe. A peaceful feeling touched the campers before they slept, the forest becoming a welcoming refuge after the storm.

CHAPTER TWELVE

The forest surrounding the shelter was dark and foreboding. Honey shivered in the night air, frightened of the environment encircling her. She did not like being left unprotected in the blackness which enveloped her. Johnathan lay in bed, eyes open, his thoughts were racing. He was beginning to understand the ways of the north. He wondered if he could survive the harsh realities of this life with no help. With that thought, he drifted off to sleep. He would not awake until the birdsong announced the birth of the dawn's early morning light.

Johnathan pulled himself out of bed, stirred the still hot coals in the fireplace, and added more wood. The mornings this far north could be damp and cool anytime during the summer. The fireplace warmed the room, taking the chill out of the air. Chase was waiting patiently by the door of the shelter for Johnathan to let him out. Shortly after he did so, loud consistent barking could be heard coming from Chase. Johnathan grabbed his rifle and went to investigate.

A hundred feet from the cabin, Chase had found a porcupine in a tree. The dog was aware of this creature which carried a protective coat of quills wrapped around his body. Chase had been on the receiving end of a painful encounter with this animal and now knew to keep his distance. Johnathan called his dog back to the shelter, allowing the porcupine to continue his journey home.

Before returning to his cabin, Johnathan decided to take Chase and hunt for some more wild game. Procuring enough food to keep one's stomach full was difficult due to the lack of refrigeration. Any wild game shot had to be cleaned and cooked the same day or smoked or salted to avoid spoilage. Johnathan had decided to spend one more day at the shelter. Any meat they shot could be cooked and smoked over the hot coals of the campfire before returning to his cabin.

After a brief time in the forest, Johnathan shot four game birds. One was a Canada goose, which he had come upon flying into a small lake which crossed his path. On their way through the woods, Chase, who was in front of Johnathan, started barking, letting him know he had found something. As Johnathan approached, he noticed a flash of white. A chill ran down Johnathan's spine, knowing what he saw was a human skull.

Upon closer inspection, it was a full skeleton, dressed in the tattered clothes of a trapper. The skull had a bullet hole in the cranium; the gun responsible for this injury laid alongside the bones. Johnathan surmised this was the previous owner of his cabin. One winter day, this lone man either took his own life or died from a horrible accident. The truth would never be known.

Johnathan decided not to disturb the remains, leaving

the man to rest in peace. Hunting lost its allure after this discovery. Johnathan returned to the shelter with the meat he had shot and the memory of a sight he would never forget. This unforgiving land had taken another victim.

CHAPTER THIRTEEN

The small shelter sat alone in the dark forest, a refuge for the man and dog who were inside. The warm glow of the burning wood in the fireplace was the only sign of life, as Johnathan and Chase were in a peaceful sleep, their concerns forgotten until waking the next day. Honey was uneasy. She knew at any moment she could be a meal for one of the dangerous predators which lurked in the dark forest surrounding her. She would be glad to return to the cabin where there was a secure structure she felt safe in.

Johnathan woke as the sun was making its daily foray over the horizon. The bright rays of the sun penetrated the windowpane on the shelter's only window. Shining in Johnathan's face, it woke him from his peaceful slumber. Chase remained settled comfortably in front of the fireplace, not yet ready to wake up. His dreams of pulling a sled through deep snow would become a reality in just a few short months.

Johnathan rolled out of bed onto the floor. He grabbed an unsuspecting Chase and squeezed him with a big bear hug. The dog returned the love with big wet kisses slobbered all over Johnathan's face. In the Yukon, one's most trusted and best friend is his dog. Maintaining a warm and loving relationship with this animal leaves one with a trusted companion who can be depended on for survival. Arriving back at the shelter after finding the skeleton yesterday, the birds Johnathan had shot were cooked and eaten for dinner. The leftovers from that meal were now being consumed for breakfast.

The trio would return to Johnathan's cabin today. Honey would have the opportunity to eat her fill in a fine meadow on the way. Honey's back was loaded with Johnathan's belongings and the party left for home. Johnathan was pleased with the outcome of this trip, confident of being successful in trapping fur if he followed the ways of the wizened man before him.

On their travels home, the group were followed by unwelcome visitors. A pack of wolves had picked up the sweet scent of Honey and were pursuing their interest in her. They followed at a safe distance until the cabin came into view. The wolves never displayed the courage for a confrontation with Johnathan and his gun.

The cabin was just like they had left it, with no signs of any unwelcome intrusions. Johnathan lit a fire in the stove to boil water. The coffee he had packed in with him from Dawson was almost gone, and he wanted to enjoy one of the last cups in his cupboard. He would resupply the coffee, if it were available, when he returned to Dawson. He needed to take Honey to town in the fall, where she would be boarded this winter.

The comfort of the cabin was offset by a constant hunger in Johnathan's stomach. The search for food was a constant reminder of the challenges he faced every day. Johnathan felt he was on a quest he did not even understand.

CHAPTER FOURTEEN

An icy wind swept through the open cabin window; a front had arrived during the night bringing with it cold air from the north. Johnathan was not ready to get out of bed. He closed the open window and grabbed a large blanket he kept for such an occasion. Snuggling under his warm blanket, he comfortably fell asleep until Chase's slobbery tongue on his face woke him. The dog needed to go to the bathroom and could wait no longer. He roused Johnathan out of his sleep to open the door and let him outside.

Once he was out of bed, Johnathan stayed awake. He let Chase outside and watched him as he relieved himself on his favorite tree. The dog then went about his morning routine, sniffing around the cabin and the surrounding area smelling for new scents left by animals during the night. After his duties were fulfilled, the dog returned to the cabin for breakfast, a meal he expected but did not always get.

Johnathan thought today would be a good day to explore Chase's skills in the canoe. His previous owner had told Johnathan the dog did well in a canoe, accompanying him on numerous trips on the water. Chase and Johnathan walked to the lake, where Johnathan retrieved the canoe from under the aspen trees and launched it into the water. While holding the canoe steady, Chase was able to board the small craft, positioning himself in the bow and keeping still. Johnathan pushed the canoe into the lake and from the stern of the canoe paddled along the lake's shoreline.

Migratory birds back from their winter vacation filled the pristine waters of the lake. Large fish swirled at the top of the water as the canoe passed their location. Reaching the far end of the lake, Johnathan noticed a beaver dam which seemed to stretch for miles. He docked his canoe on the shoreline, where the duo exited the craft. Walking along the earthen structure, Johnathan marvelled at the architecture and workmanship of these busy mammals. He hoped some of the beavers living here would end up in his traps this winter.

Johnathan decided to take Chase back to the cabin. He found it would be too awkward to fish with Chase in the canoe, as the dog had a hard time sitting still if Johnathan was not paddling. Johnathan returned Chase to the cabin, retrieved his fishing gear, and with his rifle he used for small game he left the cabin in a quest for food. He paddled the boat to a promising spot he had seen earlier in the day. Johnathan's intuition was right about fishing here. Within a half hour he boasted a catch of four nice size fish. Moving on toward the beaver dam, he managed to shoot two ducks which flew too close to his canoe. With an ample supply of food for himself and Chase, he returned to the cabin. The man and his dog would eat well tonight, a luxury few men enjoyed in this land which gave up little.

CHAPTER FIFTEEN

Man assumes nature will provide food to the hungry but only the will to survive will make this assumption come true.

The campfire, its coals glowing with high heat, cooked the wild ducks Johnathan had shot. The smell of the cooking meat made Chase's stomach ache in its desire for food. Keeping a hungry dog fed was not an easy task, as Johnathan was finding out. He cooked the fish over the fire then divided the food up between himself and Chase.

The outside air was clean and fresh. A wind blowing from the south had kept the temperature warm as night fell. An orchestra of singing crickets filled the night air, sending a symphony to reverberate through the woods. Johnathan stared at the night sky, the moon and stars gazing back at him. These celestial objects cast a light over his cabin, illuminating his home in a twilight-like darkness. This was a moment Johnathan cherished. It cemented his desire to be here in the Yukon and at that moment he knew in his heart this life would continue to be his.

Johnathan called Chase and they retired to the cabin. The inside of the cabin was warm, affording Johnathan the option of letting the stove stay cold for the night. As bedtime neared, Johnathan heard what sounded like hoofbeats walking across his yard. He went to the open cabin window and peered outside. A small doe, a female deer, had stopped to eat grass in his front yard. Johnathan could not believe his luck, fresh meat delivered to his front door. He reached for his rifle and with a steady hand he shot the deer through the open cabin window. The animal fell, dying instantly from a bullet through her heart.

As the night was warm, Johnathan thought he should immediately butcher the animal. He would cook and smoke all the best meat and leave the rest of the carcass in the forest. The predators living nearby would find the remains shortly after they were abandoned.

Johnathan dragged the deer to the fur shed and butchered it by the light of the coal oil lanterns. He had started a fire in the outdoor firepit earlier, and within an hour the coals would be ready for cooking. Dawn was breaking as the last of the deer meat cooked on the fire. The smoke from the meat attracted an unusual predator, the king of the north, the most feared animal in the Yukon.

The wolverine sulked in the dark woods. His stomach was empty, and he needed food, even if he had to take a risk to obtain it. Chase did not warn Johnathan of this menace because he did not smell the wolverine. Without warning, the feared animal rushed Johnathan's cooking area, stealing a large piece of meat and escaping into the bush with its prize, unscathed.

For a moment Johnathan was unsure of what animal so brazenly raided his cookfire and stole his meat. The lingering smell of the animal meant only one thing; it was a wolverine who passed through Johnathan's camp. This first encounter with this animal would be sealed in his memory forever. Unlike future meetings he would have with this solidary creature while fur trapping, Johnathan would never get this close to a wolverine again. This was not a disappointment he would fret about, as this animal was the most dangerous enemy he would encounter while in the wilderness of the Canadian Yukon.

CHAPTER SIXTEEN

Johnathan was up early. It was a beautiful sunny day and he wanted to take the canoe and paddle the circumference of the lake. The government representative who had prepared his deed for the cabin told him two different lakes could be accessed through connecting waterways. Johnathan wanted to investigate this claim and see if this man's story was true.

The water was calm, making the canoe launch an easy task. Johnathan left the shoreline and said goodbye to Chase, who was staying at the cabin. Chase would rather stay home, as sitting still in the canoe was difficult for Johnathan's canine companion. The canoe slid aimlessly across the placid lake. Johnathan paddled the craft slowly, taking in the shoreline, looking for anything of interest. He paid attention to areas where he observed game birds congregating, as these locations would be popular for hunting in the fall. Migratory birds would stop at his lake for rest and feed before continuing their journey south.

Johnathan's excursion took him to the farthest end of the lake, where he found a river flowing from a connecting body of water. He entered this passage and in less than half a mile found himself on another lake. Water and forest were all that Johnathan could see while paddling the canoe forward. This deep lake was surrounded by a rocky shoreline, unlike the water Johnathan lived on, which was shallow with marshy areas.

As he continued paddling, something caught Johnathan's eye; it was the remnants of an old cabin. Surprised he guided the canoe to shore to investigate. An old dock, rotten with age, lay decaying in the water. He guided his canoe into a small opening in the overgrown foliage, pulled it on shore, and walked towards the abandoned cabin. A raven complaining about Johnathan's presence squawked loudly from the roof as he approached the front door.

Entering the cabin, Johnathan was not surprised at what he saw, a building which had seen better days. Nothing of value could be salvaged from this structure. He returned to his canoe disappointed he hadn't found anything of interest and decided to head home as his arms were tiring from paddling.

Just as Johnathan was about to enter the connecting waterway to his lake, he noticed a plume of smoke rising skyward from the distant shoreline of the lake he was getting ready to leave. Johnathan was excited at the prospect of other humans nearby. He turned his canoe around and paddled to where he saw the smoke. He would have to travel across the entirety of the lake to get there. He wondered who these strangers in the wilderness could be.

After a thirty-minute journey in the canoe, that question might be answered. Johnathan hoped for an amicable greeting when he confronted the stranger in the forest, a surprise they were also not expecting.

CHAPTER SEVENTEEN

Johnathan paddled toward the shore where he saw the smoke rising upward into the sky. The blue waters of the lake stretched before him. With each stroke, the canoe drew closer to its destination, until the smoke from the campfire blew into Johnathan's face. He pulled his canoe on shore, the smell of cooking meat greeting his senses. He placed his canoe beside two others which were already sitting there.

Johnathan yelled out a greeting to the people in the bush. His call was answered with a response from a man, who told Johnathan he was welcome to enter their camp. Two Indigenous men were standing to greet Johnathan when he entered their campsite. The men explained they were a hunting party, who had come from their summer camp. The men were smoking fish and deer meat they had obtained before heading home. They told Johnathan their camp was located ten miles away, accessible by canoeing through a chain of lakes, including one overland portage.

Johnathan invited the two men, whose names were Iron Eagle and White Feather, to his cabin for an overnight stay. The men accepted this invitation, telling Johnathan they knew where his cabin was located. Iron Eagle had known the fur trapper who previously lived in the cabin and would visit him occasionally. He knew the man had disappeared and was surprised to learn Johnathan had found the trapper's skeleton in the bush.

Iron Eagle told Johnathan they would come to his home for dinner and share their food with him and Chase. Johnathan left the men's camp happy with the outcome of this chance meeting in the forest. He launched his canoe and paddled the long way back to his cabin, where Chase was waiting on the shoreline. Johnathan's dog did not like to be left alone and was happiest when he was at Johnathan's side.

Iron Eagle and White Feather arrived at dinner time. Johnathan had started an outdoor fire for ambience while the group ate dinner. The Indigenous men shared their smoked venison and fish with Johnathan and Chase. After dinner, the men sat around the firepit, engaged in conversation. The sky was darkening as the men finished eating. The wood in the fire crackled and popped, sending sparks into the night sky. The evening was quiet, with the lonely song of the loon echoing across the silent waters of the dark lake being the only sound which could be heard.

Iron Eagle and his friend decided to sleep outside by the campfire. The night was warm, and the sky was a mosaic of stars shining brightly down upon the cabin and surrounding area. Johnathan and Chase retired to the inside of the cabin and were soon asleep. Johnathan's company was leaving early in the morning to return home to their village. A surprise was in store for Johnathan tomorrow, a life changing event he never expected.

CHAPTER EIGHTEEN

Iron Eagle and White Feather were awake at dawn. The air had turned colder during the night prompting Iron Eagle to restart the fire which had burned down to ashes. Upon hearing the commotion outside the cabin, Chase woke Johnathan from his peaceful sleep. He wanted to be let outside to join the men who were now awake. Johnathan begrudgingly sat up and exited the bed. He let Chase out and yelled at Iron Eagle he would get dressed and join them outside momentarily.

Once dressed, Johnathan joined the two men who were now enjoying the warmth of the fire they had restarted. The two visitors extended an invitation to Johnathan to visit their encampment before the end of the summer months. The men had an interesting proposition for Johnathan, which they would discuss on his visit. Johnathan's decision could have a huge impact on his life moving forward.

Thinking about making the trip to the native's summer camp, Johnathan decided to take Honey to Dawson and board her. He had previously spoken to a woman named Bev, who had a large barn with six stalls ready for any wayward donkeys needing a place to stay. Honey would stay with Bev while he visited the Indigenous village with Chase. As for his dog, Chase would have to find a comfortable position in the canoe and put up with the agony of sitting still for long periods of time. With this plan in mind, Johnathan told the men he would visit within a month. He listened intently as White Feather gave detailed directions on the best route to get to their encampment while sketching it on a piece of birch bark. The Indigenous men stood from their sitting positions and shook hands with Johnathan in a friendly farewell gesture. Johnathan watched as the men paddled their canoes out of sight.

Anxious to go visit his newfound friends, Johnathan began to prepare for his journey to Dawson. He was not sure how long Honey would be staying in town but knew she would be safe at Bev's. Johnathan prepared for his trip to Dawson, planning on leaving in the morning. Evening came quickly, with the waning sun projecting another dark night in the forest.

Johnathan sat around the campfire, feeling lonely, as he had no human companionship. The starless night added to the darkness of his mood. He was hungry, not having eaten since Iron Eagle's gift of food the previous evening. On the way to Dawson, his chances of successfully hunting for food would increase. He felt certain both he and Chase would be able to eat their fill tomorrow.

Johnathan's sleep was restless that evening. He was becoming uncertain if he was on the right path, as the dangers of living alone in the bush increased his chances of dying prematurely. Johnathan decided he would follow through on his planned trip to visit his new friends, after which he would decide whether he was going to stay the winter in the bush and trap for fur or return home to California. His dreams that night were about his life in the wilderness. Would the draw of the north be enough to keep him here in the Yukon or would he head back to California where life would be easier? Only he could make that decision.

CHAPTER NINETEEN

The blanket lay crumbled at the bottom of the bed near Johnathan's feet. He rolled, reached for it, and pulled it up over him. Chase, noticing Johnathan was awake, jumped onto his bed, a morning ritual that both man and dog enjoyed. Showing companionship and affection towards one another was the primary reason for this routine.

Today Johnathan was leaving for Dawson, with Chase and Honey accompanying him on the journey. He retrieved Honey from her barn and loaded the supplies needed for the trip to Dawson on her back. A short time later, Johnathan was securing his cabin and getting ready for his departure. It was a warm sunny day as the trio headed into the bush. After a short distance they entered a lush meadow where Honey was given time to eat. She ate the tender green grass until her stomach was full.

As they continued their journey, Johnathan shot two squirrels and a rabbit. As both he and Chase were hungry, he decided they would stop early for the night to allow him to clean and cook the food to satisfy their perpetual hunger. The group travelled until mid afternoon and stopped to camp at a lake they were familiar with on the route to Dawson.

Johnathan knew there was a healthy population of fish in the lake from his previous stay here. If he was successful fishing later, he knew they would have food for tomorrow.

The blue waters of the placid lake shone like a polished diamond. Johnathan set up camp and collected firewood for cooking. He cleaned his prey and prepared the meat, placing the savory food on the fire when the coals glowed red. The smoke from the cooking food drifted into the surrounding forest. Chase sat patiently by the fire waiting for the wild game to cook. What seemed like an eternity later, dog and man happily shared the meat. The hunger Johnathan and Chase had been living with was temporarily subdued by this meal.

After eating, Johnathan went to the lake with his fishing gear. In a brief time, he had three fish on shore. He also shot a duck which flew too close to his gun while leaving the lake. Johnathan left his fishing spot and returned to camp. He gathered more firewood, cleaned the fish and the duck, and cooked the meat over the fire. He did not finish until late into the night, the sun setting hours earlier.

A hungry fox lurked in the shadows hoping to enter Johnathan's camp later for any mislaid food left behind. The night was black, as a heavy cloud cover had moved in obscuring the moon and stars. Johnathan drifted off into a peaceful sleep. Upon awakening the trio would continue their journey to Dawson, dropping Honey off at her temporary home. Johnathan and Chase would return to their cabin where Johnathan would plan his trip to the natives' camp. He was anticipating this visit, which could change the course of his life. Johnathan hoped the proposition would be a good one, but that may not be reality.

CHAPTER TWENTY

Johnathan's eyes opened. He had heard movement in the dark forest which bordered his camp. He lay still and listened for any more sign of activity. Chase had picked up the scent of lurking danger, causing a low growl to come from deep within the dog's throat. Johnathan felt for his rifle, which he kept close. He knew a predator in the forest was waiting for the opportune time to attack and drag Honey off into the dark woods.

Honey was beside herself. She was in a panic knowing a large animal in the woods wanted to eat her. Silence fell over the forest as Chase waited for an imminent attack from this hidden danger. The dark clouds which had previously filled the night sky had moved on, leaving a mosaic of stars shining down on Johnathan's camp. This light allowed him an advantage in the fight he was about to wage for Honey's life.

Suddenly, Johnathan heard the crashing of a large animal running toward their camp. A black bear appeared out of the forest, intent on making the donkey his dinner. With one well placed shot, Johnathan's bullet hit the bear in the heart. The animal staggered forward towards Honey, collapsing in death feet from the terrified animal.

Johnathan's heart raced as he relived this horror in his mind, realizing how close he had come to losing Honey to this hungry predator.

Johnathan dragged the dead bear off into the forest, deciding he would deal with its body in the morning. He returned to camp and comforted his nervous animals. Johnathan lay on his back looking skyward, unable to sleep after this disturbing encounter. An infinite universe stretched before his eyes. Eventually, the sun returned as a globe of light in the early morning sky. Johnathan got up and dressed the bear. The cool night air had helped preserve the meat, allowing him to pack the choicest cuts to take with him to Dawson. The rest of the carcass would be left for scavengers to fight over.

The trio prepared to leave, with Johnathan expecting to reach Dawson by late afternoon. He found irony in the fact that Honey was packing the remnants of the bear which tried to eat her. He would deliver the meat to the Mounties in Dawson, who would distribute it to townspeople who could benefit from such a find. The group walked the shoreline until it meandered its way back into the forest. The day passed quickly, and the travelers made good time.

The afternoon was waning as the buildings of Dawson City came into Johnathan's view. After dropping by the Mounties' office to drop off the bounty of meat, he headed to the livery stable to leave Honey overnight. He would plan for the donkey to stay at Bev's later. Johnathan told the livery owner the animal was hungry, as Honey had not found food she liked on the trail to Dawson. He said he would pay for extra feed and hay, in addition to the boarding fee in the morning and then headed to the hotel with Chase. He planned to spend two nights in town.

The proprietor recognized Johnathan from his last stay, when he purchased Chase, and was glad to see him return. He told Johnathan fresh beef was on the dinner menu, along with his wife's fresh baked bread and hot apple pie. He also told Johnathan he had some good food for his dog, and a large moose bone for Chase to chew on for dessert. Johnathan thanked the proprietor for his hospitality, telling him he would be down later for dinner but first wanted to head to his room.

Johnathan, with Chase in tow, climbed the stairs and unpacked his bag. He removed his clothes, climbed into bed and drifted off into a peaceful slumber, unintentionally sleeping through the night. It was early morning when the sound of gunshots coming from downstairs abruptly woke him. The silence which followed cast uncertainty over Johnathan's once happy spirit. He quickly got dressed and headed downstairs to see what happened, fearing a robbery had taken place.

CHAPTER TWENTY-ONE

Johnathan and Chase descended the hotel stairway to the lobby below. He could see the Mounties talking to the innkeeper, who was standing behind the front desk. Johnathan and Chase, both now ravenous as they had slept all night, walked to the dining room to eat breakfast. After sitting for a brief time at a table, the proprietor's wife approached with a menu. Johnathan ordered food for himself and Chase and inquired about the gunshots which he heard earlier. The woman explained two ruffians passing through town had robbed her husband. The gunshots had been a warning, fired into the ceiling of the hotel by the bandits. A small amount of money had been taken in the robbery and the culprits had fled Dawson, escaping into the wilderness.

Johnathan ate a generous portion of bread, pork, and eggs for breakfast. Bread baked in a large oven at the hotel was always a mouth-watering treat to look forward to when lodging here. Served throughout the day, the breads' reputation for excellence was known all over the territory. The innkeeper's wife also prepared food for dogs, stew made from leftovers was always available for them. Johnathan and

Chase finished their meals and left to visit a local native woman named Bev.

Bev lived on the outskirts of Dawson and boarded livestock in a barn her nephew had built on her property. Johnathan had met Bev when he was previously in town and knew a young woman helped her manage the livery business. He hoped she would have space for Honey to stay with her. Upon arriving at Bev's cabin, Johnathan and Chase were warmly greeted by its hospitable owner. Bev did indeed have room for another animal and showed Johnathan the barn where Honey would stay. The stall was clean and free of manure and an abundant supply of food was on hand for the animals to eat. Boarding Honey at Bev's barn was costly, but Johnathan knew his donkey would get the best of care here. Johnathan told Bev he would retrieve his donkey from town and bring her later this afternoon.

Johnathan left Bev's house happy with the arrangements he had made for Honey's care with this kind woman. Chase and Johnathan walked back to the livery stable to pick up Honey. Upon arriving at the stable, Johnathan paid the bill for her lodging and headed back to the donkey's new home. The trio soon found themselves back in the barn, with Honey being shown her new accommodations. A feeling of joy spread over Honey, as the donkey realized she would be safe in the secure barn. After the horrifying encounter with the bear, she had no desire to live in the wilderness again. However, Johnathan would be the one to make that decision. not Honey.

As Honey looked around her new home, she had her eyes on a handsome donkey in the next stall. His name was

Omar. He was the most popular donkey in the barn and the favorite of the girl who cared for the animals. A friendship between these two donkeys would flourish, a friendship that would turn into love and end in an unexpected pregnancy for Omar and Honey.

CHAPTER TWENTY-TWO

T he chirping birds woke Johnathan, while his dog was still asleep. Loud, boisterous activity from the street below caught his attention and woke Chase. Johnathan sat up in bed and then moved to the window. In the early morning dawn, he watched two Mounties trying to control a man who appeared to have had too much to drink. The two constables told the man he would be spending the day in a jail cell for public intoxication. When he had sobered up, he could return home to his wife and children.

The man arrested for public drunkenness was a native. Unfortunately for the natives, the gold seekers and fur trappers who had flooded the Yukon had introduced liquor to the Indigenous population. The white men used alcohol as a trading or bargaining tool and often cheated the natives out of their furs and food. Called firewater, it devastated Indigenous families and their ways of life. Addiction ruled over common sense, leading to many needless deaths in their tribes. Trying to keep alcohol out of the hands of the native people was a formidable task.

Johnathan and Chase were leaving Dawson this morning. They would travel with only the things needed for this journey and a handful of supplies. Johnathan hoped the return trip to his cabin would be problem free. After eating breakfast at the hotel, Johnathan purchased food from the innkeeper for himself and Chase. The duo left Dawson with full stomachs and a healthy attitude.

The first part of the trail from Dawson was used by many travellers. Most of these wayward men were searching for gold. Unfortunately, hundreds of helpless souls would end up dying in their quest to find this precious mineral. The bones of these dead men would be bleached white from the Yukon sun in the remote sites where they perished.

The day was hot, with the temperature going up to ninety degrees. Sweat poured from the brows of both man and dog. After veering off the main trail, the duo reached the lake where they would camp for the night. Chase was dehydrated and weak, glad for a drink of cold lake water upon their arrival. Johnathan set up camp by the lake. After dusk when the temperature dropped, he lit a campfire. The fire cast light over the surrounding area, making it easier for Johnathan to see. He sat by the campfire with Chase, both travelers hungry. The food they had carried from Dawson had spoiled from the heat. Johnathan threw their dinner out, not wanting to get sick from eating spoiled meat. He would hunt for game tomorrow and, if successful, they would have food when they returned home.

The sky shone with countless stars; the campfire was but a dim light in a vast universe. The fire burned down, its dying embers prompting Johnathan and Chase to sleep. As they slept, eyes watched from the forest. Chase woke as an unusual scent invaded the dog's nostrils. A low growl from

Chase woke Johnathan. Alarmed he reached for his rifle, sensing danger. A skunk-like smell invaded his senses.

The sky had darkened, and the campfire had burned out. Johnathan listened, his senses heightened by the silence and darkness of the forest surrounding him. The silence was broken by something crashing through the dense underbrush in a bid to leave the area. Silence followed with no explanation as to what had just happened. Did Johnathan and Chase have an encounter with Bigfoot or was it just a nosy bear? The dark forest was the only witness, and the truth would never be known.

CHAPTER TWENTY-THREE

The sound of distant thunder woke Johnathan and Chase from their uneasy sleep. Dawn was like a shadow, the rising sun obscured by the dark thunderclouds which filled the early morning sky. Johnathan cursed himself for not buying jerky while in Dawson. The easy availability of food for both he and his dog from the hotel made Johnathan forget how hard it was to feed himself and Chase. He had mistakenly left Dawson with the wrong food on a hot day. Johnathan learned his lesson the hard way; the best way to remember your mistakes, which could cost you your life.

The man and his dog broke camp early and moved forward along the trail. With a brisk walk Johnathan hoped to reach his cabin by early afternoon. The skies darkened with approaching thunderheads and loud thunder and flashes of bright lightning filled the turbulent sky. Johnathan and Chase needed to find shelter from the storm. A loud barking led Johnathan to Chase's location. He had found a den which had been used by a bear for winter hibernation. Johnathan cleared debris from the entrance and entered the opening of the abandoned den.

Inside, the duo stayed dry from the storm which sent

torrents of rain and flashes of lightning overhead. The storm passed, taking the loud thunder away to a distant sky to repeat this act of nature over again. As the storm passed, the sun came out and glistening raindrops fell from the tallest trees, a reminder of God's handiwork.

As Johnathan and his dog continued their journey, the heavy rain had made the trail muddy, slowing their progress. Johnathan noticed large, hoofed tracks in the mud on the trail; a moose was walking ahead of them, also using this highway in the forest. This animal was off limits to shoot in the summer due to the inability to preserve the meat after the animal was butchered. Johnathan placed Chase behind him and picked up his pace. He was hoping to see the moose, who with a full rack of antlers was the most majestic animal of the north.

A short time later, Johnathan caught sight of what he was looking for. The adult male moose had moved off the trail and was up to his underbelly in a grassy marsh, eating to satisfy the hunger in his stomach. The rack of antlers on his head rose above the grass for all the forest animals to see. Johnathan continued to his cabin leaving the moose to eat, hoping their paths would cross this winter under a different set of circumstances.

Three hours later, Johnathan's cabin came into view. Approaching the front door, Johnathan noticed one of the extra boards he had used to reinforce his front door had been pulled out and left hanging. He surmised a black bear had tried to get into his cabin but had failed in the endeavour. Johnathan was glad to be home but ready for his next adventure, the trek to Iron Eagle and White Feather's summer camp.

CHAPTER TWENTY-FOUR

As Chase and Johnathan entered the cabin, a rush of hot air greeted them. Johnathan opened the windows to let some air circulate throughout the interior of the building. He had noticed the wind direction had shifted to the north and hoped by tomorrow morning the heat would be replaced by cooler air.

Hunger gnawed away at the stomachs of both man and dog. No game had been shot on the return trip from Dawson, as the oppressive heat had kept the animals from being active. Their only movement in the forest had been to find water and a cool place to sleep. Johnathan's plan was to catch fish for dinner by taking the canoe and paddling to his favorite fishing spots. With luck, the man and his dog would end the evening with full stomachs.

The lake was calm, the placid waters reflecting the trees which hugged the shoreline. Johnathan reached the first area he wanted to fish and loaded his hook with grubs and worms he had dug up from around the cabin. He had also collected bugs, frogs, and other aquatic creatures from the pool at the freshwater spring. With this bait, he caught enough fish for dinner and was back at his cabin to a joyous Chase within two hours.

Johnathan gathered firewood and started the cooking fire. By the time he cleaned and prepared the fish, the coals in the fire were ready for cooking. A hungry fox, smelling the fish, waited in the shadows for an opportunity to steal a portion of the remains for himself. Johnathan cooked the fish over the open fire, the delicious aroma drifting into the forest. The waiting fox was crazy with hunger.

The full moon shone down on Johnathan's homestead. He had noticed the lurking fox in the treeline. The parts of the fish which Johnathan found unusable were fed to the hungry fox. The animal's patience had been worth the wait. Johnathan and Chase enjoyed their meal, filling their stomachs, allowing for a good night's sleep. There was even fish leftover for tomorrow's journey.

In the morning, Johnathan and Chase would leave their cabin and journey by canoe to the Indigenous encampment in the forest. Before reaching the location, it would be necessary for them to portage the canoe and camp for one evening. Johnathan planned arriving midday to Iron Eagle's camp, hoping his friends would be present and not on a hunting trip.

As the fire's coals burned down, the sky darkened with clouds blocking the light from the moon. Johnathan and Chase retired to the cabin, tired and ready to sleep. The silence of the night sent them into a peaceful slumber until the morning sun roused them for another day.

CHAPTER TWENTY-FIVE

The cabin sat alone by the lake as the spirits of the night were awakened. A mysterious sound echoed across the quiet water; an unidentified song often described as haunting. It was the call of the loon, a unique bird sacred to the Indigenous tribes of North America. During the summer months, this aquatic species lives in the northern lakes, with a call which sounds like no other. Sitting by the lake late at night, the wailful song of the loon captivates the listener. The call from this bird is an unforgettable experience, a special sound which returns to the minds of all who hear it, reminding them of special moments spent in nature.

Johnathan's eyes opened. Through the cabin window he observed the first rays of light casting shadows over the landscape. Johnathan had already packed the supplies he could carry for the trip he was about to embark on. After little preparation, Johnathan and Chase were ready to leave the cabin. Johnathan secured the cabin door with extra boards, not knowing when he would return. He made his way to the lake with Chase in tow.

Retrieving the canoe, Johnathan loaded Chase and his

belongings on the craft and pushed the canoe away from shore, jumping on board before getting wet. Johnathan paddled the canoe across the calm water of the lake, the map White Feather had drawn for him within reach should he need it. Johnathan paddled across the vast expanse, his canoe a small dot on this large body of water.

With Chase sitting quietly in the front of the canoe, they arrived at the passage leading to the next lake they had to transit. Johnathan decided to stop at a small island in the middle of the channel connecting the two lakes. Chase needed a bathroom break and to stretch his cramped legs. Here the pair would share the leftover fish for lunch.

After a one-hour break, Johnathan and Chase continued their journey. The next stop would be at the portage, a well marked trail which led to another lake. White Feather told Johnathan it would take him about an hour to carry his canoe and supplies across the small strip of land which stood between the two lakes. As planned, Johnathan arrived at this destination before dark. He would make camp here tonight and do the portage tomorrow, after a restful night's sleep.

As he neared the shore, Johnathan was pleased with the progress he had made today and with Chase's behaviour in the canoe. Tomorrow he would arrive at his destination. Would Johnathan be ready for the changes which were about to happen in his life? Only time and his destiny would tell him if he made the right choice, a decision he would live with forever.

CHAPTER TWENTY-SIX

When the canoe hit the shoreline, Chase jumped from the boat onto dry land and immediately ran to the nearest tree to relieve himself. The dog then went about investigating his surroundings. Finding nothing of interest, Chase returned to where Johnathan was setting up camp. Finishing collecting wood for the campfire, Johnathan completed the chores he had to do and his thoughts shifted to food for dinner. He took Chase and his rifle to hunt for small game in the surrounding forest.

Johnathan and his dog walked the portage trail until they reached the next lake, where the pair would continue their journey tomorrow. They sat quietly on the shoreline of the water when a sudden noise caught their attention. The long grass lining the bank of the lake rustled with movement. Johnathan aimed his gun toward the activity, waiting for the suspected waterfowl to show themselves. Two ducks soon appeared and, without warning, both were shot by Johnathan. This lucky break in hunting for food meant the pair would eat meat for dinner tonight.

Distant movement on the lake caught Johnathan's attention; a canoe was being paddled in his direction. As the craft drew closer, Johnathan recognised the two men aboard as Iron Eagle and White Feather, the men whose village Johnathan was on his way to visit. A surprised greeting took place with warm handshakes exchanged between the three men. The men explained to Johnathan they were fishing for the tribe and their village was three hours by canoe from this location. Before leaving, Iron Horse gifted fish to Johnathan and Chase for dinner. The men left telling Johnathan they would see him tomorrow.

With their food issues solved, Johnathan and Chase returned to their camp on the other side of the portage. Johnathan started the fire so the food they had gathered could be cooked. Dusk settled into the forest, followed by the blackness of night. The food sizzled, cooking on the hot fire. Johnathan and Chase ate their fill and then lay by the fire. The comfortable environment soon sent them both into a deep sleep.

The following morning, Chase was up first. He nuzzled Johnathan, as if to say he was ready to continue their journey. After eating leftovers for breakfast, Johnathan began the portage. He carried the canoe first, followed with his supplies. One hour later, everything was on the shore of the next lake and Johnathan and Chase were ready to start the last part of their trip. Chase took the bow, seating himself as comfortably as possible in this small space. Johnathan paddled from the rear, while the supplies were packed in the middle of the canoe. Their travel would take them across the middle of the lake to the village on the other side, where their journey would end.

CHAPTER TWENTY-SEVEN

Johnathan paddled his canoe across the calm waters of the lake. The cloudless sky and bright sunshine caused beads of sweat to drip from his brow. Johnathan disliked crossing these large northern lakes by canoe because if caught far from shore in a storm his chance of survival was slim. Large waves caused by high winds could capsize the canoe, throwing him into the water where hypothermia and drowning would cause death.

Johnathan scanned the sky for any sign of bad weather; only the bright sun and cloudless blue sky stared back at him. Chase slept peacefully in the bow of the canoe. The horizon stretched indefinitely, with no land in sight, as Johnathan paddled the canoe across the large lake. The only signs of life were Canadian geese flying overhead, their loud honking informing him of their presence. Johnathan's arms were tiring, as the length of the crossing was strenuous for one man with a paddle. He set the paddle down in the canoe to rest his arms, when a sudden bark from Chase made Johnathan look up. A distant shoreline greeted his view, causing him to pick up his paddle and resume his trip across the lake.

An hour later, Johnathan could see the smoke of campfires burning. He steered his canoe in the direction of the smoke, visible above the trees in the forest. When the canoe drew closer, Johnathan could see children and their mothers on the shoreline. The people waved a friendly greeting at Johnathan when he landed his canoe on the small beach they were standing on.

The appearance of two smiling men set the tone for the visit. Iron Eagle and White Feather held out their hands in greeting, big smiles on their faces. Johnathan and Chase were glad their long canoe trip was over. The men carried Johnathan's canoe to where the tribes' own canoes were located. With White Feather leading the way, the men walked toward the village the tribe had set up in the forest. Chase was approached by the dogs living with the tribe. Johnathan felt Chase needed to have skirmishes with these dogs as they worked out how to exist together. If the alpha dog of the group felt Chase was going to be submissive, he might be accepted into their pack.

The camp was large with thirty residents who were all family members. Many in this group were women and children. Johnathan noticed numerous campfires burning, which were being used to smoke meat the hunting parties had returned with. Smoked fish hung between trees, suspended on rope which these innovative people had crafted from vines.

Iron Eagle informed Johnathan a large celebration would be held this evening, to honour their new friendship. Feasting, drum playing, singing, and dancing would be part of the festivities, which would culminate with an announcement by the Chief. This proclamation would hopefully change Johnathan's perception of the north, giving him a reason to stay in the Yukon and provide hope for his future.

CHAPTER TWENTY-EIGHT

The celebration was to start at sundown, a special event which would be presided over by Iron Eagle's father, Chief Rising Sun. He planned to offer his daughter, from his much younger second wife, to Johnathan for marriage. A refusal of this proposal would be an affront to the chief, banishment from the forest the result if Johnathan did not accept the chief's offer. Johnathan was totally unaware of this plan, a surprise he would not learn about until the evening's festivities ended.

As the skies began to darken, all tribal members gathered around a large fire. The people living in the village had been told to dress in full tribal regalia for this event. Food was served, which included a generous supply of fresh and smoked deer meat and fish, accompanied by edible greens and roots from plants which grew in the forest. A delicious tea, made from the leaves of a common plant, helped wash down this hearty meal. Drum playing, dancing, and singing by tribal members followed the meal.

As the midnight hour neared, all festivities stopped. Silence fell over the people as the chief took centre stage. He asked to be joined by his daughter and Johnathan. The chief took each of them by the hand, and looking at Johnathan, told him he was offering his daughter to him for marriage. She was older and experienced in the ways of her people. She would join him in his cabin and teach him how to trap and hunt for food. With Shining Star as his wife, his chances of survival in the Yukon would now be possible. The chief said their union would be a way of welcoming Johnathan into the family.

Johnathan graciously accepted the chief's offer to take his daughter as his wife. A wedding was set to be held under the next full moon, which was a week away according to the tribe's calendar. Until that time, Johnathan and Chase were expected to live with the tribe. After the ceremony, Johnathan would then be accepted as a tribal member.

After being roughed up by the alpha male, Chase was accepted into the dog pack and had made friends with the other canines. These dogs were part of a much larger pack which were used as sled dogs during the winter months. Only the calmer dogs accompanied the tribe to their summer camp. The rest of the pack remained at the permanent village which was located south of their present location. The elderly members of the tribe stayed behind to look after matters there while the younger members traveled to hunt and fish.

Johnathan was nervous about the upcoming wedding. He was not sure what the bride's father expected of him. Taking the chief's daughter in marriage could not be taken lightly by the new groom, who wanted to be accepted into the tribe. A knot grew in Johnathan's stomach, as the wedding was tomorrow. His honeymoon would include taking his new love away to a life in his cabin. When he began this journey, he never thought he would return home with a new wife and an improved outlook for his future. A future he could now share with someone he loved.

CHAPTER TWENTY-NINE

The preparations for Johnathan and Shining Star's wedding were extensive. Chief Rising Sun was meticulous about planning this one-time event involving his only daughter. Using greenery from the forest, the venue was decorated for the ceremony. Fires cooking fresh meat for the festivities burned throughout the village. Dinner was served first, a variety of fresh meat cooked to perfection for the guests to eat. After dinner was finished, drum playing and dancing took the stage. As the night wore on the festivities continued.

The full moon shone brightly on the ceremonial grounds where the wedding was to be performed. Chief Rising Sun appeared, raising his hand and calling for quiet from the people. He asked for Johnathan and Shining Star to approach him. Johnathan, dressed in native attire, followed Chief Rising Sun's directions, standing before the chief with his future wife by his side. The marriage ceremony was conducted by a tribal elder, who joined the young couple. He prayed that a happy future would follow the couple as they struggled together for survival in this unforgiving wilderness, called the Yukon.

The party continued till the first light appeared on the horizon. This was a sign from the heavens to end the wedding festivities. The people in attendance returned to their homes to sleep. A special teepee had been erected for Johnathan and his new bride to sleep in. The young couple fell in love on their wedding night, a romantic night in the teepee consummated their marriage. Their love for one another was a match called perfection.

The following morning it was time for the young couple to leave for Johnathan's cabin. Shining Star would paddle her own canoe loaded with her belongings and supplies she felt they might need for the trip. The send off from the village was a special event for the tribe. All the members came to the beach to say goodbye and wish the couple luck for their future.

After bidding her family goodbye, the couple paddled in silence. Johnathan's plan was to travel across the lake with the two canoes to the portage. Following their arrival, they would move their canoes and supplies to the next lake the couple needed to cross. They would make camp when this work was done.

The lake crossing was uneventful, the couple finding themselves at the portage without any mishaps. They moved their belongings across the land bridge to the lake on the other side. Johnathan wanted to leave early in the morning, hoping to arrive at his cabin before dark tomorrow. With their work completed, Shining Star lit the campfire while Johnathan collected additional firewood. They ate dinner, which Shining Star had brought from the village. After dinner, they lay on their backs gazing upward, a million shining stars looked back at them. The couple slept the night wrapped in each others' arms, a growing love blossoming between them.

CHAPTER THIRTY

Johnathan awoke shortly after midnight. The warmth of the afternoon and early evening had been replaced by cooler nighttime air. He grabbed Shining Star's hand, pulling her up off the ground. After stoking the hot coals in the fireplace, Johnathan added more wood. He retrieved a blanket and the couple laid down beside the fire covering themselves. The newly wed couple snuggled under the warm blanket, comfortable laying together under the dark northern sky. They listened to the sounds originating from the forest.

The sound of the hoot owl looking for his mate and the cry of the wolf pack announcing a kill were two of nature's musicians which could be heard emanating at night. Perhaps the most recognised song came from the lake, a low soulful orchestra of sound echoing across the silent water, the call of the loon. A spiritual and sacred bird to the native people, the birds' message in song was a symbol of hope in a difficult land for the people who settled here. The loons' songs left an echo in listeners' heads, which will settle into a corner of their minds forever.

Birdsong filled the air when Shining Star awoke, the

bright rays of sunshine in her eyes. It had been a restless night for the couple; sleep was fleeting. They awoke tired but ready for the day. After breakfast, the canoes were loaded with the couple's belongings. Chase, with a full stomach, resumed his position sitting in the front of Johnathan's canoe. The couple left the portage, paddling toward Johnathan's cabin. They crossed the first lake and stopped for lunch on the island in the channel which divided the two lakes.

Johnathan noticed many freshwater clams in the water near the shoreline. The couple gathered a sack full of these shellfish for dinner. After eating a lunch of smoked deer meat, they continued their canoe trip across the vast lake. Three hours later, a bark from Chase signalled land was ahead. Johnathan looked up, pleased to finally see the shoreline. In one hour, they should be at his cabin. He was looking forward to showing his wife her new home, a cabin where they would start their life together, a place to share their love forever.

Johnathan's beach soon came into view and a brief time later both canoes were pulled ashore. The boats were unloaded; the couple's possessions were placed on dry land. Johnathan took his wife's hand and turned her body to face the lake. He told her he wanted to name this lake their cabin sat on in honour of her father. The Lake of the Rising Sun would be a metaphor for his presence, always there for her when his love was needed.

These were the ways of the north, where nature takes the lead and man's presence becomes just part of the experience, a lesson that Johnathan would soon learn.

CHAPTER THIRTY-ONE

Johnathan removed the extra boards from the outside of the cabin door. Used to strengthen the door to keep predators from entering the cabin, Johnathan left the door this way if he was going to be away from home for more than two days. He opened the cabin door and Shining Star entered her new home. A smile broke out across her face, knowing this cozy cabin was the beginning of her new life with Johnathan. The atmosphere was warm and inviting. Chase stood beside Shining Star, whining and rubbing against her for attention. She reached down and rubbed the dog's back lovingly.

Shining Star told Johnathan she loved the cabin and felt lucky to have married such a proud man. Johnathan went outside to let Shining Star get acquainted with her new home, while he began carrying their things from the lake to the cabin. As Shining Star worked inside the cabin organizing their belongings, Johnathan gathered firewood to build a fire to cook the shellfish they had collected earlier in the day. Once these chores were completed, Johnathan gave his bride a tour of the rest of the property.

Johnathan showed his wife the spring where they could

collect fresh water for drinking. Water for most other uses came from the lake, an unlimited source of fresh water, even in winter. A hole in the ice kept open by the occupants of the cabin provided a guaranteed water source all winter. If the spring froze, water from the lake could be boiled and used for drinking. Shining Star was surprised by the outbuildings, especially the fur shed. Johnathan's home was more than she ever hoped for.

The wood from the outside fire was soon crackling, the smoke drifting skyward joining the wispy clouds in the darkening sky. Evening was approaching as Shining Star, Johnathan, and Chase sat outside by the fire. The shellfish, boiled in a large pot of water, were consumed by the hungry newlyweds. The couple decided this delicious meal was all they needed for dinner and returned to the cabin. Johnathan lit another fire inside the woodstove to help take the dampness out of the structure. The warmth which spread throughout the structure created a feeling Johnathan had been missing since he left the cabin to retrieve his new wife.

As darkness crept over the land, the spirit on the lake announced itself with song. The loon, calling for his mate, was a distinct sound which would be repeated throughout the night. The loon's various melodies would echo around the lake, but never give up its secrets.

The beginning of July was here, officially recognized as summer. The month of July and the first two weeks of August were typically the warmest months in the Yukon. Temperatures could reach ninety degrees and vicious thunderstorms could sweep through the area during this time of year. Outside the cabin, the couple could hear the winds growing stronger and the rumble of thunder in the distance. Shining Star closed the windows in the cabin, anticipating a storm was coming. The winds intensified and flashes of lightning accompanied by loud thunder surrounded the couple's cabin. Trees could be heard crashing to the ground in the forest, blown down by strong wind.

Safe in their cabin, the couple lay in bed listening to the dissipating storm, the lightning now a distant threat. A peaceful sleep, accompanied by the fresh air from the now open windows of the cabin, overtook the young couple. The forest was quiet, still recovering from the storm. The morning sun would bring change and mark the beginning of another day.

CHAPTER THIRTY-TWO

Johnathan suggested to Shining Star they take a trip to Dawson. They would pick up Honey, Johnathan's pack animal, who was being boarded at a stable near the edge of town. The donkey would carry new stove pipes from Dawson City back to the cabin, as Johnathan needed to replace the old pipes on the stove before winter came to the Yukon. He also wanted to buy new saws for the wood cutting which needed to be done. A large supply of firewood was needed for the woodstove, as the brutality of the cold Yukon winter made having enough wood for the season a priority. Burning all available fuel early, meant certain death.

The couple decided to leave for Dawson early tomorrow morning, but today they were taking Shining Star's canoe out on the lake together. The larger of the two canoes allowed this Indigenous woman the opportunity to show Johnathan how to use a net to catch fish. The summer day was beautiful as the couple launched the canoe into the pristine blue waters of the lake. They paddled in unison to a deep part of the lake. Shining Star took the fish net she had brought with her and placed it in the water. Johnathan maneuvered the canoe following his wife's instructions. After a brief period, Shining Star started to retrieve the fishing net from the water, which held four large whitefish. Johnathan was surprised at how effective this method of fishing was compared to using a line and bait.

Shining Star told Johnathan this method of fishing could be used under the ice during the winter. She had brought two fishing nets which had been made by the elder women of her tribe, a handicraft which was already being forgotten by some of the younger members. She was glad she had learned how to make and repair such nets before marrying. Johnathan felt this way of gathering food could be a life saving option when no other means were available.

The couple finished fishing and organized the canoe for a sight seeing trip on the lake. They paddled in unison, Johnathan taking his wife to the beaver dam at the marshy end of the lake. Shining Star was surprised at the size of the dam and the number of beavers living in the area. She told Johnathan they should benefit financially, trapping these valuable fur bearing mammals this winter. An abundance of waterfowl lived at the lake. Returning in the spring from their winter vacation, the birds nested and raised their young here during the summer months. This meant eggs were plentiful in the spring and fresh duck and geese were available all summer to eat.

After a short tour of the large lake, the couple returned to the cabin. Johnathan cleaned the fish, feeding some of the remains to Chase. He disposed of the inedible fish parts by placing them back in the lake for the scavengers to eat. While there, he washed up and then joined his wife in the cabin for a nap. The couple were happy together enjoying their new life in their little cabin in wilds of Canada's north.

CHAPTER THIRTY-THREE

Shining Star lay awake in bed, while Johnathan, still asleep, lay beside her. The morning sun shone through the open window, casting its warm glow throughout the interior of the cabin. Shining Star shook Johnathan to wake him. Rising from the bed, she opened the cabin door to let Chase outside. She called out to Johnathan again to wake up, as she began to pack supplies they would need for their trip to Dawson. Johnathan persuaded himself to get out of bed and help her with this job.

The preparations for their trip were soon finished. The couple sat at the table and ate smoked venison for breakfast, while Chase was fed leftover whitefish from dinner the night before. With full stomachs, the three embarked on their trip to Dawson. The day was sunny and warm and the route they travelled was an easy walk. The day passed by uneventfully and by late afternoon they reached the lake where they would camp tonight. Their campsite was on a high point of land which overlooked the lake. The beautiful view of the surrounding area overwhelmed the young couple. After a dinner of fresh fish, Johnathan and Shining Star lay beside the fire. This is where they slept, wrapped tightly in each other's arms.

Johnathan and Shining Star rose early. The couple sat on an outcropping of rock and watched as the sun rose over the horizon. The reflection of the sun on the still waters of the lake was a memorable sight. After eating a quick breakfast, the trio was off on the second leg of their journey. Johnathan expected to reach Dawson by late afternoon. They would stay at the hotel which was familiar to him and tomorrow would buy the stove pipes and other supplies needed for the cabin. They would pick up their pack animal from Bev and board her at the livery stable in town for the night, allowing them to leave early the following morning to make the trip back to the cabin.

The time in Dawson passed quickly and soon the couple found themselves at Bev's stables picking up their donkey. Johnathan introduced Shining Star to Bev. After a brief conversation between the two women, they realized they were related. Bev was Shining Star's great aunt through marriage. Bev told her surprised great-niece she had other relatives living in the forest nearby and the donkey which was stabled beside Honey was owned by her cousin, Wendy, and her husband Jason. Shining Star was even more surprised to learn she had a one-year-old cousin named Kuzih. Bev told her Wendy's brother, Steward, who raised sled dogs and trapped fur, also lived nearby.

Johnathan was shocked to learn of all the relatives Shining Star had living in the area. Bev told Shining Star she would let her relatives know another family member was living in the forest nearby. The couple gathered up Honey and said their goodbyes to Bev. They told her they would return Honey in the late fall to spend the winter.

Honey would have a much easier life during the winter than the one Johnathan and Shining Star were facing in the bush, a reality which would come sooner rather than later.

CHAPTER THIRTY-FOUR

Early the following morning, Johnathan and Shining Star picked up Honey from the livery stable. They walked to the hardware store where the owner was a big man with a barrel chest and a hearty laugh. He had sold Johnathan the last set of stovepipes he had in his store, along with the saws needed for cutting wood yesterday. After securing their purchases on Honey's back, they left Dawson for the cabin.

Travelling with Honey made for a slower pace on the trail, but Johnathan felt they could still make the trip with just one overnight stay. The hot July sun beat down on the party as they slowly trudged towards home. Finding a green patch of grass, Johnathan decided to stop for lunch and let Honey graze. The rest of their group found a large shade tree on the edge of the meadow and gathered under it to cool off and rest. They ate lunch, then continued their journey. Johnathan wanted to reach the halfway point back to his cabin today, reaching the lake before dark was a priority for him.

The sun was setting when the group arrived at the lake. The couple set up camp and lit a fire for some light. They ate some of the smoked meat they had purchased in town for dinner. The campfire was but a speck of light in the dark forest. The crackle of the burning wood and the call of the loon from the lake were the only sounds to be heard. Johnathan and Shining Star sat around the fire watching the hot flames burn the wood, lost in a world unlike their own.

The sound of distant thunder abruptly changed their thoughts. Luckily, the rain stayed a distance away, leaving them dry for the night. The couple fell asleep by the campfire snuggled comfortably together under a blanket. Upon awakening in the morning, they ate the rest of the jerky they had travelled with. They broke camp and left immediately after breakfast, hoping to get to their cabin before darkness settled in.

It was dusk when the cabin came into view. Johnathan unloaded the materials from Honey's back and placed her in her barn with fresh water and grass he had gathered during the early summer. Then he joined Chase and Shining Star in the cabin. The air had cooled during the early evening and now blew in through the cabin's open windows. Tired from their trip, the couple's sleep was peaceful, their dreams about their future. It was a life they could call their own, a tiny piece of forest in a land the natives called paradise.

CHAPTER THIRTY-FIVE

The summers in the Yukon are short and preparations for the winter season start early. During the cold winter months, the material used to seal the cracks between the logs of the cabin becomes crumbly and falls out. This results in small holes which allow cold air from outside the cabin to enter. Having cold draughts coming into the cabin during the winter months requires burning more wood to keep the space warm. Sealing these cracks before winter arrives is a necessary job for the owner of the cabin to undertake. This was the project Shining Star was going to work on today while Johnathan changed the stovepipes in the cabin.

The couple awakened to a warm sunny day. Chase waited anxiously by the door to be let outside. A pair of blue jays, a bird common in the forests of the Yukon, sat on a branch outside the cabin window. The couple watched as the birds broke out in song, as if greeting the couple with a wake-up call. The bed was warm and comfortable. Johnathan and Shining Star were in no hurry to change positions and start another day, until a sudden barking from Chase caught their attention.

A man's voice could be heard talking to Chase.

Johnathan and his wife, realizing they had a visitor, got out of bed and dressed quickly. A knock at the door and a greeting by the man outside, made Shining Star realize it was her brother, Iron Eagle. She opened the door, hugged him tightly, and invited him into the cabin. Iron Eagle had brought the couple gifts of coffee and food. Johnathan put water on the stove to boil. He would prepare coffee for everyone, an uncommon drink living in the wilderness of the Yukon.

Iron Eagle told Shining Star he felt a need to check on his younger sibling. He was also there at her father's request. After a lengthy visit, Iron Eagle, with the promise of returning another time, left to return home. He would be happy to report Shining Star was doing well when he saw their father. The siblings tearfully embraced when saying goodbye.

The work on the cabin was started shortly after Iron Eagle left. The fire was allowed to go out and the pipes were given time to cool before Johnathan could replace them. In the meantime, the couple worked together on chinking the logs to seal the cracks to make it draught proof. One hour later Johnathan was able to replace the stove pipes with new ones he had purchased in Dawson. After successfully completing his job, Johnathan helped his wife finish sealing the cracks.

The day had been hot and long, and the couple were tired and sweaty. Night had fallen as the newlyweds and Chase headed to the lake for a swim to cool off. The full moon shone down on the swimmers and the cold northern waters chilled their bodies to the bone. Back at the barn, a terrified Honey sensed a predator outside her enclosure looking for a way to enter. The smell of the donkey sent the bear into a lustful rage. Honey shrieked in warning, alerting Johnathan to the danger. Johnathan grabbed his rifle and ran naked towards Honey's enclosure hoping he was not too late.

CHAPTER THIRTY-SIX

Johnathan ran toward the shed where Honey was kept. As he approached, he observed a bear in a frenzy trying to break into the structure. The animal was so fixated on what he was doing, he did not notice Johnathan coming up behind him. This gave Johnathan time to decide if he would shoot to kill the bear or shoot to scare the animal back into the forest. He raised his rifle and shot the bear in the head at close range. The young bear fell dead on the ground, his short life taken by a predator called man.

Johnathan returned to the lake where he had told Shining Star and Chase to stay while he investigated the issue with Honey. Shining Star laughed at Johnathan's nakedness. He jumped into the cold lake water to cool off once again. After his swim, the couple with their dog returned to the cabin. Johnathan needed to check on Honey and deal with the body of the bear. Honey was still shaking in fear from her close encounter with death. Johnathan rubbed the animal's back, consoling her the best way he knew how. Honey wished she was back at the barn in Dawson where she knew she was safe. She missed her new friend, Omar, who kept her from feeling lonely. Honey had come to adore this handsome donkey; his sense of humor and charm kept her swept off her feet.

After calming Honey, Johnathan drug the bear away from the front of her enclosure. When he returned to the cabin, Shining Star had made coffee. The couple discussed butchering the bear tomorrow and smoking the best parts of the meat for future consumption. The full moon shone its bright light down upon the cabin, making the surrounding forest feel innocent but a lurking predator in the bush had caught the scent of blood.

The wolverine made its way toward the unsuspecting inhabitants of the cabin. The smell of blood was strong, allowing him to find the dead bear and feast on it. His presence would not be known until the morning, his stealth and silence winning him a free meal. The following day, Johnathan was ready to butcher the bear. Shining Star built a fire, as the couple planned on smoking the meat. Johnathan had taken the bear a distance from the cabin, not wanting to attract additional predators to Honey's enclosure. When he got to the bear, he was shocked at what he found. Large parts of the bear had been eaten during the night.

Johnathan called Shining Star over to have a look at the bear. She told Johnathan it was a wolverine, fur trappers' number one enemy. This animal would need to be extinguished from their territory before the start of the trapping season. Its ruthless ability to disrupt and destroy could lead to a loss of up to fifty percent of the fur on the trapline. Shining Star told Johnathan they would set a trap and kill the wolverine before it could inflict such damage.

For now, the wolverine with its full stomach, survived

to see another day. Johnathan started butchering the bear and two hours later had cut all the meat from the carcass he wanted to save. He took the harvested meat from the bear and gave it to Shining Star to cook and smoke, leaving the remains for the scavengers to feed on. That bear had provided a generous supply of meat which would keep the group nourished, a gift from nature hard to replicate.

CHAPTER THIRTY-SEVEN

Using the meat harvested from the bear, Shining Star decided to prepare a stew on the woodstove in the cabin. She had gathered plants from the forest and added the greens she had selected into the stew. Fresh vegetables were a rare commodity in the bush and the plants Shining Star collected were a good substitute for root vegetables typically found in stews. As dusk approached, Johnathan finished smoking the bear meat, while Shining Star tended to the bear stew.

The couple decided to go to the lake and watch the sunset before dinner. The water was calm and their mood was relaxed, as Shining Star rested her head in Johnathan's lap, savoring the love she felt for this man. Small waves lapped the shoreline as a sudden breeze blew across the lake. The sky darkened as dusk descended upon the forest. Upon returning to the cabin, the savory aroma of the bear meat lit up the couple's senses. Chase was waiting, whining with anticipation, for his dinner. After the food was devoured, the couple retired outside and lit a fire. It was a beautiful evening, with a sky full of stars shining brightly down on them.

The wolverine lurked in the darkness. The bear meat he had feasted on was gone and the remains of the animal had been carried off by a pack of wolves. The smell of the bear stew had caught his attention, drawing him to the cabin. He watched as Johnathan and Shining Star enjoyed the campfire and the evening together. Without recourse, the wolverine slinked away back into the forest. He would now treat the cabin as a food source, returning when the odour of cooking food caught his attention.

The couple watched the sky, wishing on the shooting stars which lit up the dark night. Chase lay quietly by the fire, enjoying spending time with Johnathan and Shining Star. The embers from the fire glowed in the darkness as the remaining wood burned, exhausting its fuel. The tired couple and their dog returned to the cabin to go to bed. The night had turned cool, as the wind direction had changed, now blowing briskly from the north.

The cabin was warm and inviting, as its three residents found comfort in their own beds. The call of the loon echoed across the lake, a soulful wail which would never be forgotten by its listeners. Surviving in the Yukon was becoming a reality for Johnathan and his new wife, Shining Star. She felt the spirits which watched over her people would also watch over them. The couple's dreams were pleasant and peaceful throughout this northern night. However, a disquieting incident tomorrow would upset the calm, casting the couple back to where they really belonged, in the wilds of Canada's north.

CHAPTER THIRTY-EIGHT

The loud call of a raven outside their open window, woke the couple from their undisturbed sleep. The first light of the morning sun was evident through the window, as Johnathan and Shining Star lay in bed awake. The raven's persistent call echoed throughout the cabin. Johnathan rose from the bed and shooed the bird away, then opened the cabin door to let Chase outside. Johnathan returned to bed to his waiting wife, who was not ready to get up. She took Johnathan in her arms, hugging him tightly. Peace fell over the cabin as the couple drifted back to sleep.

Chase's barking woke the couple from their comfortable slumber. Johnathan pulled himself out of bed to see why his dog was barking. He opened the cabin door and heard a squirrel, not happy with the dog's presence, chattering at him from a branch high up in the tree, causing Chase to bark loudly. Johnathan called his dog, telling him to come back inside.

Today, Johnathan and Shining Star would take Honey and complete maintenance work on the two emergency shelters on the trapline. They would pack enough supplies to sleep overnight at the shelter at the far end of their route. The structure abutted a large beaver dam, meaning the couple could travel no further. Before departing, Johnathan secured the cabin, taking extra precautions because of the wolverine's presence on their property. If this animal were to gain access to the inside of their home, the wolverine would destroy or damage the contents of the cabin while looking for food.

With Johnathan leading Honey, they walked the worn trail of the trapline. In the forest, a wolf pack gathered, the scent of donkey overpowering their senses. The wolves were planning an attack. Chase alerted the couple to the danger, whining incessantly. Anxiety gripped the couple, who sensed something was wrong. The forest grew silent, indicating an attack was imminent by an unknown enemy. With their firearms ready, Johnathan and Shining Star waited for their adversaries to show themselves.

Out of the bush appeared the wolf pack, confident and unafraid. They stealthily approached their prize; Honey's odor combined with their hunger caused them to let their guard down. The sound of gunfire erupted, breaking the silence. Three of the animals lay dead from the barrage of bullets unleashed on them. The remaining members of the pack retreated into the cover of the forest. The dead animals were left to lay where they died, their bodies would be picked clean by scavengers.

Johnathan's group reached the first shelter, where they stopped to eat lunch. After a short stay, they travelled to the last shelter and began work, upgrading the building for the winter trapping season. They would spend the night here before returning to the first shelter tomorrow, completing upgrades on that building before returning home. For now, safety and shelter from the elements was the goal, comforts sometimes not given in this unforgiving land.

CHAPTER THIRTY-NINE

The upgrades on the shelter were completed before dark. Johnathan decided to sleep outside with Honey, as an attack by a predator was likely if she had no one protecting her. Shining Star lit a fire outside the shelter. The night air in the Yukon can be cool even during the summer months. The night was dark, a cloud cover obscuring the light from the stars. The couple sat around the fire drinking coffee Shining Star had prepared for them. The Canada geese living in the beaver pond suddenly started honking loudly, the loud song indicating there was danger in the area. Most likely, it was just a fox looking for dinner.

The cloud cover cleared from the night sky, leaving a mosaic of stars for the couple to view. Shining Star decided to join her husband in sleeping outside, as the night was pleasant and dry. The wolverine had followed the entourage from their cabin this morning and had kept the couple within his sight all day. He also thought Honey would make a delicious meal. However, the wolverine knew his chances of making that dream come true were slim to none.

The group slept peacefully under the stars and the morning sun shone brightly as it rose over the horizon.

Johnathan and Shining Star stood from the hard ground they had slept on all night. They ate a quick breakfast and left the shelter with Honey in tow. The wolverine followed the group from a distance. He enjoyed stalking them, looking for an opportune moment to rip the throat out of Honey and enjoy her tender meat.

After three hours on the trail, the foursome reached the shelter closest to the cabin. They repaired the door which had been left hanging when a bear broke into the shelter looking for food. Johnathan nailed down some loose shingles on the roof while Shining Star filled cracks in the logs to keep out the cold air this winter. With their work here completed, they headed home.

Walking the trail, Johnathan noticed a stiff breeze had developed and the rumble of thunder echoed in the distance, indicating a storm was approaching. The couple knew they had to seek shelter and found some large trees uprooted in a previous storm, leaving their roots exposed above ground. Other trees had fallen on top of these large root structures, providing a sheltered area in which to escape some of the heavy rain that was about to fall. The storm unleashed its fury upon the group as they huddled together. The heavy rain poured through the shelter, soaking them to the bone.

The storm soon passed, and the sun reappeared, its warmth welcomed by the now cold travellers. One hour later, their cabin came into view. Glad to be home, the couple stripped off their wet clothing and built a fire in the wood stove. The cabin was damp and cold from sitting empty while they were gone. Only the call of the loon was heard from the lake, as a silence gripped the cabin, the little structure the couple called home.

CHAPTER FORTY

The month of July had turned into August. Johnathan and Shining Star had discussed taking Honey back to Dawson, returning her to Bev's stable where she would be safe from the predators living in the bush wanting to eat her. Honey would stay with Bev until late September, when Johnathan would use Honey to carry supplies to the cabin before winter. After that trip, the couple would return her to Dawson where Honey would spend the winter in Bev's barn.

Johnathan and Shining Star decided to leave in the morning, to head to Dawson. The trip to town was without incident, with fine weather and no predators. Their first stop was Bev's place to drop off Honey. When they arrived at Bev's house, Shining Star's cousins, Wendy and Jason, were there with their baby. They had come to pick up Omar, their donkey, who was going to carry supplies to their cabin. After a joyous meeting between the two couples, Johnathan talked to Wendy about acquiring two sled dogs from her brother.

Steward raised sled dogs on his property in the bush. Shining Star had told Johnathan they would need two more dogs to pull the sled this winter if they were going to work the trapline together. In the spring, the two dogs would be returned to Steward for boarding over the summer. Wendy told Johnathan she would make arrangements with Steward for the purchase of the dogs. If he and Shining Star travelled to her cabin in mid-October, she would take them to meet Steward and pick up their dogs.

Everyone was happy, except Honey. The handsome donkey she had been looking forward to seeing was leaving with Jason and Wendy. Omar would not be returning to Bev's barn until late in the fall. Honey would have to wait until Omar returned for the winter to spend time with him. However, she was glad to be here at Bev's, away from the dangers in the forest which haunted her wherever she went.

The group of relatives said their goodbyes, reminding each other they would see one another in a couple of months. Johnathan and Shining Star left for the hotel, where they would be staying in Dawson. After checking in with the friendly proprietor, the couple, along with Chase, went to their room. A large window overlooked the street, allowing the couple entertainment watching as the drunken patrons staggered out of the saloon across the way.

Johnathan knew the hotel was noisy, but it was clean. Bedbugs and cockroaches infested the other hotels in town. The couple lay on the bed wrapped in each other's arms. Sleep followed until the dinner bell rang downstairs, summoning the couple to the dining room. What was on the menu tonight? A delicious bear stew.

CHAPTER FORTY-ONE

A loud crash followed by yelling woke Johnathan and Shining Star from a deep sleep. It was after midnight and two patrons from the bar across the street were fighting over a gambling debt. Johnathan walked to the open window and closed it, watching as the Mounties arrived to help settle the dispute. Johnathan returned to his wife waiting in bed. The saloon closed shortly after this unfortunate incident took place, allowing the couple to sleep comfortably for the rest of the evening.

Johnathan and Shining Star awoke to the smell of frying pork downstairs. They decided to eat a hearty breakfast before leaving on their return trip to their cabin. With Chase in tow, the couple walked downstairs to the dining room. They ordered a portion of meat to be added to a bowl of dog food for Chase. The dog had not been eating well since they left the cabin with Honey for their trip to Dawson.

After eating a large breakfast, the couple returned to their room and gathered up their belongings. They settled their debt at the front desk, thanking the friendly owner for his hospitality. The group left Dawson, with Chase leading the way. They reached the edge of the forest shortly after leaving town. It was a two day walk back to the cabin from Dawson. During the winter, with the dogs they planned to purchase from Steward, Dawson would become a one-day trip on the sled if the weather was good.

Today, Johnathan would be happy if they made it to the lake where they usually camped before nightfall. The lake was the halfway point between Dawson and their cabin. The day was sunny with a cool breeze, the August weather in the Yukon bringing cooler mornings and earlier sunsets. At the end of the month, changes would begin as nature readies itself for winter. The deciduous trees, proud and green all summer, will become dormant, their brightly coloured leaves drifting aimlessly to the forest floor.

After a day with no mishaps, the couple reached the lake. To Johnathan's surprise, another couple had set up camp there. The couple had travelled from Vancouver to Dawson and from there, they had travelled by canoe through interconnecting lakes until they found themselves here. They told Johnathan and Shining Star they were writing a story for a magazine called the *National Geographic*. Their story was going to be about the Canadian North and the people who lived there. The writers wanted to interview Johnathan and Shining Star about their life in the Yukon.

The new friends ate dinner together, as Johnathan and Shining Star answered many questions about their lives. This chance meeting in the forest was welcomed by both couples and would be memorialized in a story published in the magazine, something Johnathan and Shining Star were proud to be a part of.

CHAPTER FORTY-TWO

Both couples were awake early and enjoyed a cup of coffee together. They watched the sun rise over the lake. Johnathan and Shining Star ate a quick breakfast of beef jerky, which they had purchased in Dawson. They shared this food with their new friends, who were grateful for their kindness. With hugs and good wishes, the couples parted ways, heading in different directions.

The August sun was warm and the trail to the cabin was long. Dusk was approaching when they neared their destination. Chase was thirsty, going to the lake for a drink of cold water. Johnathan opened the cabin door, and, with Shining Star, they entered the cabin. The couple were tired from their long walk and were glad to be home. Johnathan looked out the window of the cabin. He could see the moon rising over the lake, the beauty of the moment catching his attention.

Shining Star told Johnathan her father believed serene happenings were good for the human spirit. He told her when the loon's song pierces the stillness of the night, the soul feels at peace with the spirits of the north.

Johnathan called Chase to come inside the cabin, as

he was aware a wolverine could be prowling around the property and an unexpected run-in with him could lead to Chase's death. The dog was no match for this ferocious animal, who would rip his prey's throat out with its powerful jaws. Shining Star lit a fire in the woodstove to make coffee for Johnathan and her. Smoked bear meat was for dinner. The bear meat had been placed in a glass jar and sunk into the pool of frigid water at the spring. This method of refrigeration was a way to help keep the meat from going rancid, extending its shelf life for a few more days.

After dinner, the couple headed down to the lake, holding hands as they walked. They were pleasantly surprised to see a deer drinking from the water. Johnathan spared the animal's life, knowing they might need the meat during the winter months when food was scarce. Watching the sky for shooting stars, the couple made wishes for their continued happiness. The moon shone with a brilliance which illuminated this desolate northern lake. A feeling of love for one another washed over the couple as they lay in each other's arms.

The couple returned to the cabin. The outside air had turned cool, and the cabin was warm and comfortable. The couple retired to bed earlier than usual, as the days were beginning to grow shorter and darkness fell sooner in this land called the Yukon, where only the strongest survive.

CHAPTER FORTY-THREE

Chase was awakened by a noise in the middle of the night; an animal was on the roof of the cabin. The faint odour of wolverine caught the dog's attention. The predator on the roof was looking for a way inside. Johnathan was awakened by the same noise and woke Shining Star, telling her to listen. She heard footsteps on the roof of the cabin as well. Johnathan grabbed his rifle and walked toward the door. He did not want to confront this dangerous animal in the middle of the night, so he would just shoot his gun into the sky to scare off the intruder. A direct confrontation with this dangerous mammal could end badly.

Sensing activity inside the cabin, the wolverine froze, allowing silence to fall over the building. Johnathan opened the cabin door., raised his gun in the air, and pulled the trigger twice in quick succession. The deafening sound of gunfire echoed throughout the forest. The footsteps of the wolverine running to get off the roof were heard by the couple. Calm was restored in the cabin, as Chase returned to his favorite spot by the woodstove and Johnathan returned to bed with his wife.

The wolverine was becoming annoying, and Johnathan needed to come up with a plan to end this problem as soon as possible. He would talk to Shining Star in the morning about coming up with a solution to end the animal's stalking behaviour. The forest surrounding the cabin was quiet and the occupants inside were soon sleeping again.

Birdsong filled the early morning, as the sun was rising. Johnathan slid out of bed, leaving Shining Star to sleep. He dressed and went outside with Chase. The mid-August mornings were getting noticeably cooler, and today a chilling wind from the north greeted the pair as they stepped outside the cabin. Johnathon thought today would be a good day to prepare their outside freezer for the winter. The winter freezer was a small room built under the ground, near the cabin. It is used in the winter to freeze and store meat from large kills, such as moose and deer.

The morning sky was crimson red. Johnathan walked the short distance to the lake, where he sat and watched the waterfowl fly onto the lake looking for an early morning meal. Johnathan laughed as Chase waded into the lake, taking a bath. Johnathan stood up and returned to the cabin alone, Chase would stay outside till he was dry from his swim.

Johnathan quietly got back in bed with Shining Star, who was still asleep. He lay beside her, wrapping his arms tightly around her. She responded by turning to face him and kissing him deeply. Chase's scratching at the door to be let back into the cabin was ignored by this passionate couple, who were too busy to comply with the dog's wishes. Chase returned to the lake, lying down in the warm sunshine. He would try again later to get his owners' attention and enter the cabin. For now, he would snooze in the warm sunshine for an hour, his dreams being his only concern.

CHAPTER FORTY-FOUR

Chase's loud barking woke Johnathan and Shining Star from their sleep. When the barking didn't stop, Johnathan cursed at his dog under his breath and rose to investigate what the noise was about. He pulled his clothes on and walked to the lake, where Chase was sitting, staring out over the water. Johnathan looked and observed a canoe in the distance, moving toward the cabin. Johnathan estimated whoever was paddling the craft would arrive in about an hour.

Returning to the cabin, Johnathan told Shining Star a visitor was coming. She wondered if it was her brother, Iron Eagle again, or perhaps her younger brother, White Feather. Shining Star rose from the bed to ready the cabin for a visitor. She started a fire in the wood stove to heat water for coffee. The couple had just enough of this valued commodity for this morning. Johnathan went back to the lake to wait for the man approaching in the canoe. As the boat got closer to shore, Johnathan identified the occupant of the boat as Iron Eagle.

Upon greeting each other, a solemn look spread across Iron Eagle's face. Asking to speak with his sister in private, Johnathan remained at the lakeshore. A short time later, Shining Star left the cabin, sobbing uncontrollably. She found Johnathan and hugged him tightly. Her brother had delivered news about her father, who had suddenly become ill and died a short time later. On his deathbed, Chief Rising Sun had asked Iron Eagle to go to Shining Star and tell her his spirit would always be with her. Whenever she heard the call of the loon, she would know her father was there.

The body of Shining Star's father had been buried quickly, before decomposition could set in. Iron Eagle gave Shining Star some mementos from her father, which she would treasure forever. Iron Eagle, being Rising Sun's eldest son, would now become the new chief. He left to return to his summer camp after delivering the sad news and having coffee with his sister and brother-in-law. His new duties awaited him, as the tribe would soon be returning to their village to prepare for the winter.

After Iron Eagle left, Johnathan thought a relaxing canoe ride on the placid lake would be a morale booster and help his wife take her mind off of her father's death. Shining Star agreed and gathered her net to catch some fresh fish for dinner. The couple left the cabin for the lake and launched Shining Star's canoe into the clear waters. They paddled the craft together in unison, their speed at a fast clip.

The blue sky met the blue waters of the lake, creating an illusion of no horizon. Shining Star could feel the spirit of her father comforting her, his spirit now belonged to the lake. The couple spent half a day on the water, returning to the cabin with fresh fish and a rejuvenated spirit. Shining Star realized all life must come to an end, and it was her father's turn to join the spirits in the after life. It was a sad ending for someone who would never be forgotten.

CHAPTER FORTY-FIVE

Johnathan and Shining Star were expecting more visitors soon. Before leaving the tribe's encampment, the young couple hired two of Shining Star's family members to travel to their cabin and cut wood. A winter's supply of hardwood needed to be cut for the cabin's woodstove before the winter season. The two men's expected arrival at the cabin was the first week of September. It would take an estimated two weeks to complete this job, with Johnathan and Shining Star helping with this project.

Today's work for the couple was preparing their outside freezer, a small storage area dug out of the earth to keep meat frozen, for the winter. A wooden platform was placed over the opening to this underground freezer to keep the snow out and deter hungry animals from stealing the meat being stored there. After examining the outdoor storage area, Johnathan noticed part of one of the walls had caved in. He retrieved a shovel and removed the excess dirt which had collected on the floor. After replacing some rotten wood of the storage covering, Johnathan's work was done. The couple could start using this life saving method of storing food in early November.

For now, Johnathan needed to go hunting. With the arrival of the hired help, they would soon have two extra mouths to feed. An abundance of migratory ducks and geese at this time of year meant no shortage of waterfowl to eat. With Chase in tow, Johnathan and his dog went hunting. Shining Star stayed behind and would take her canoe to go fishing with her net, while Johnathan tried to secure meat. Johnathan was hoping to bag a young doe, which would provide an abundance of meat.

The man and his dog followed the trail of the trapline. To Johnathan's dismay, Chase ran ahead, scaring any game he came across. Aggravated with Chase, Johnathan returned the animal home and locked him in the cabin. For a second time Johnathan left to go hunting, this time without his dog. Without the animal's presence, his luck changed immediately. In one hour, he had bagged two rabbits, who had exposed themselves to the sights of his rifle.

Johnathan walked to the first emergency shelter built along the trapline, stopping here to eat a meal of smoked fish. After finishing lunch, Johnathan leaned back against a tree stump and fell asleep. The warm sun beat down on Johnathan, making him so comfortable he did not want to wake up. In a half-dream state, he imagined he heard hoof prints on the hard ground. A sudden rustling of tree branches caught his attention, causing Johnathan to open his eyes. He thought he was dreaming. Fifty feet from where he had fallen asleep, a young doe was browsing on the overhanging branches of a tree.

The deer had not noticed Johnathan sleeping, nor detected his scent. Johnathan quietly reached for his gun, as the deer, sensing no danger, continued to nibble on the boughs of the tree she was under. With trembling hands, Johnathan aimed for the deer's heart. An explosive shock from the gun silenced all wildlife in the forest. The young doe fell dead, a bullet in her heart and food still in her mouth. Johnathan was happy, this kill would supply meat for the men who were coming to cut wood. Sometimes nature provides when it is least expected.

CHAPTER FORTY-SIX

Johnathan stood up from where he had been sitting and walked the short distance to where the dead deer lay. He immediately took the knives he had brought with him from the cabin and started butchering the animal. Two hours later, the small deer was dressed. He packed all the meat he could carry on his back and would have to return to retrieve the rest.

The wolf pack had been watching Johnathan since he killed the deer and were waiting for him to leave the area. The animals would then converge on the kill sight, claiming the remains of the deer. The cuts of meat Johnathan left to pick up on his second trip, were what the wolves would eat first.

Johnathan struggled under the load of meat he was carrying, making the two hour walk to the cabin long and strenuous. Upon arriving, Shining Star was surprised to see all the meat Johnathan had harvested in such a short time. She immediately got to work, building a fire to cook and smoke the meat. Johnathan left to return to where he shot the deer to collect the remaining meat. After a long walk, he reached his destination and was shocked at what he found. The meat he had come to retrieve was gone. Wolf tracks pointed to the thieves. Disgusted by this change of events, Johnathan turned around and returned home.

Upon his arrival, Johnathan found two men helping Shining Star cook the venison. The smoker was being operated by one of the men who had arrived while Johnathan was gone. All three of them were experienced in smoking meat in the bush, a skill which had been handed down through the generations of Indigenous tribes to preserve meat. It was a cooking technique adopted by those living in the wilderness of Canada's north.

The two men had come to cut wood and introduced themselves as Josh and Rodney. Johnathan found it unusual for two Indigenous men to have white men's names. The boys' father was a white trapper who had met their mother while living in the bush. The couple married and their mother left the tribe. When the sons became men, they preferred the communal lifestyle tribal living offered, so returned to live with their mother's people.

Johnathan was glad to have the helpers there and explained to the men there were many fallen trees in the bush. These deadfalls had either blown down during storms or were diseased trees that had died and fallen to the forest floor. The plan was to cut the wood and stack it where it lay. Johnathan would retrieve it this winter, using his dogs and sled. Johnathan was paying well for the job, with a bonus when it was completed. Josh and Rodney would use the money they earned to buy supplies from the white man, making life easier for their tribe.

The four adults and Chase enjoyed fresh fish and venison for dinner. Josh and Rodney had brought supplies with them for camping and would sleep outside while staying on the property cutting wood. After eating, the new friends sat around the fire talking, but were soon ready to go to bed. Everyone retired, wanting to be well rested for cutting wood tomorrow, which promised to be hard work.

CHAPTER FORTY-SEVEN

The wolverine sniffed around Josh and Rodney's camp, looking for leftovers or food dropped from dinner the previous evening. The early morning sun was rising in a clear blue sky, waking the two campers in the tent. The wolverine found no food and noticing movement and talking coming from the boys' shelter, decided to move back into the forest where it would be safe from any firearms the predators in the tent might possess.

The boys pulled themselves up from the hard ground they had slept on. They exited their tent and played with Chase, who Johnathan had let outside earlier that morning. Shining Star, carrying a plate of smoked venison for Josh and Rodney, appeared from the cabin. Johnathan joined the trio outside and enjoyed breakfast with his new acquaintances. The men discussed Johnathan's plan for gathering the winter's wood. They would cut dry wood from dead trees lying on the forest floor, which would be stacked on site. The wood would be picked up this winter when there was enough snow for the dog team to retrieve it with the sled.

Two weeks went by before the job was done. The young men had worked hard, cutting enough wood for the cabin and the two shelters on the trapline. Johnathan paid them with cash he had taken from the bank the last time he was in Dawson. A strong bond had developed between the young men and the couple, with Rodney and Josh promising to return the following year, if they were needed, to cut wood. The morning the young men left was sad, as they pushed off their canoe from the shore leaving Johnathan and Shining Star alone once again.

The young couple returned to the cabin glad the worrisome job of finding enough fuel for the winter had been solved. The couple lay back down in bed enjoying the quiet of the forest. Wrapped in each other's arms, they soon fell back asleep. Their calm was shattered by a knock on the cabin door and Chase's loud barking. Johnathan awoke startled, got out of bed, and grabbed his rifle as he headed for the door. He asked who was knocking, grasping his rifle tightly, unsure if it was a friend or a foe. A man's voice answered, identifying themselves as Northwest Mounted Police officers from Dawson. Surprised, Johnathan opened the door and greeted the two men.

Inviting them inside the cabin, Johnathan asked the men the purpose of their visit. The Mounties told him and Shining Star an extremely dangerous man, known to police, had shot and killed a Mountie in Edmonton. Somehow the man had managed to escape a massive manhunt and weeks later was seen in Dawson. When the Mounties in Dawson moved in to arrest the wanted man, he had escaped into the bush. They knew he was familiar with the area, as he had lived in Dawson for many years in the past. The Mounties were warning people living in the isolated cabins in the forest surrounding Dawson about the danger this desperate man might present to them.

Johnathan and Shining Star thanked the Mounties, who left after delivering their news to visit the next homestead. Before leaving, the constables left some coffee for the young couple, which they were happy to get. Shining Star brewed a pot to warm up their spirits, as both she and Johnathan were now worried about this unstable fugitive living in the forest. This official visit by the Mounties was an unpleasant surprise, which left the young couple hoping the officers would soon catch this man without incident.

CHAPTER FORTY-EIGHT

One of the most popular pastimes in the Yukon in 1898 was panning for gold. Many streams and rivers which flowed through the land offered up deposits of gold flake and nuggets of varying sizes. Johnathan found gold pans stored in the fur shed and Shining Star told him about a fast-flowing stream fed by spring water less than a day's walk from the cabin. She explained the creek was well known among the Indigenous tribes for producing gold. The couple decided to take Chase and travel to the water Shining Star talked about to try their luck at panning for this precious metal. They would take enough supplies to spend two nights on the bank of the creek.

Two days later, after eating breakfast, the couple and their dog left on their journey. Johnathan secured the cabin door, knowing the wolverine would come knocking after they left. Shining Star led the procession, knowing the way to the gold-bearing stream. She had travelled there with her father many times in the past, always with good results at finding gold. The mid-September weather was cool during the day and colder at night. Shining Star's father had told her this was the best time to visit the creek to find this precious metal.

The crunch of dry leaves underfoot on the trail pointed to the onset of fall. The vegetation was brown and dying and the large deciduous trees were almost bare, their naked limbs reaching skyward. The day's journey was long but uneventful. Johnathan was lucky enough to shoot two rabbits on the walk to the creek hidden deep in the forest. During the mid-afternoon they could hear the roar of a waterfall. Drawing closer, the couple realized they had reached their destination. A fast-moving stream, just as Shining Star had described it, came in sight.

The couple found a flat area to set up their camp near the waterfall. They gathered enough firewood to keep the fire burning throughout the night. Sleeping outside with no shelter and only a blanket to cover up with promised to be cold and uncomfortable. The fire would provide the only true warmth. Johnathan cleaned the rabbits he had shot on the walk here, which would be the couple's dinner tonight. Chase would share this meal with Johnathan and Shining Star, while sitting around the fire.

The night came quickly and the fire crackled, casting light into the dark forest. The shining stars shed light over the couple's camp, as the soothing sound of the waterfall softened the atmosphere of their surroundings. An owl hooted in the forest for its mate, who was out looking for food. The trio relaxed around the fire, sharing the rabbit meat for dinner. Shortly thereafter sleep followed, the sound of the cascading waterfall sending the couple into a deep slumber until the sun rose the following morning.

CHAPTER FORTY-NINE

Chase was awake before daybreak. He went to Johnathan's side nuzzling his face to wake him up. The dog had smelled a dangerous predator lurking near their camp and needed to warn Johnathan about this hidden danger. Johnathan stirred, waking up from his sleep and reached out to scratch Chase's head. A noise coming from the forest made Johnathan realize why his dog was at his side. He reached across and shook Shining Star lightly. She opened her eyes and listened to Johnathan as he whispered why he woke her from her sleep. The couple lay still and listened as the noise grew closer. Chase whined, uncomfortable with the situation developing around him. A loud gunshot suddenly echoed throughout the forest, then another. Johnathan had decided to act first, trying to scare the predator off. The loud noise from the gunfire worked, as the retreating animal could be heard crashing through the woods.

The sun was rising over this hostile and unforgiving land. The breeze was blowing the last dead leaves off the hardwood trees, as Johnathan watched them slowly float downward, settling lightly on the forest floor. The campers ate breakfast and were now ready to try their luck panning for gold.

The couple decided to first check the pool which collected water from the waterfall. Shining Star waded into the water and skillfully did her work with the pan. Johnathan joined her in the pool, which produced poor results; only one small nugget of gold between the two of them. Not willing to give up, the couple decided to try the stream bed. They looked for pools of water which had formed in the creek bed, hoping deposits of gold had been washed into these basins by fast moving water in the spring.

Johnathan's first try at panning in the new location produced good results, four small gold nuggets appearing in his pan. Shining Star told Johnathan this creek produced mostly nuggets, as gold flake was not common in this stream. After working the stream for gold most of the day, Shining Star and Johnathan had found twenty nuggets. The value of their find was not great due to the small size of the nuggets; however, the couple deemed this venture a success and were glad to be carrying gold back to the cabin.

Smoked meat was on the menu for dinner and then another night of sleeping by the fire before heading home in the morning. The birdsong coming from the forest woke Johnathan and Shining Star early, a forest melody not repeated anywhere but in nature. The group ate the last of the beef jerky for breakfast and broke camp. A light misty rain followed the couple and their dog home, causing the trio to feel wet and cold. After a long day on a wet trail, the cabin finally came into view. This shelter would offer them a warm place to change their wet clothes and relax their tired bodies. There is no place like home, even if it was just a cabin in the wilderness.

CHAPTER FIFTY

The fluffy white clouds moved slowly across the clear blue sky. The early morning sun shone brightly down upon the desolate cabin in the forest. A light breeze blew the cool September air through the open windows. Johnathan sat up in his bed, covered Shining Star with the blanket, and then stood up and closed the open windows of the cabin to keep the chill out. Chase was waiting impatiently at the cabin door, as Johnathan went over to let him outside. Within minutes of being let out of the cabin, Chase was barking loudly.

Johnathan quickly got dressed, grabbed his rifle, and opened the cabin door. Looking where his dog was, he could see a small animal which appeared to be in distress. Walking closer, he saw a young fox with a rusted trap attached to his leg. The trap was past its prime, with the spring being unusable. Yet somehow, this young fox got his leg trapped. No injury had been done to the fox, but it was difficult for the animal to move or run away with this heavy device attached to his leg. Shining Star, hearing all the activity outside, had gotten out of bed and dressed. She came out to see if she could help Johnathan.

Putting an unwilling dog in the cabin, was Shining Star's first task. The fox was young and very scared, but seemed to sense these people were going to help him. As Shining Star talked to the fox in a warm friendly tone, the animal responded, appearing to trust her. She reached down and with no negative response from the fox, was able to free the rusty trap from his leg. Finally unencumbered, the fox did not leave. Shining Star told Johnathan she was returning to the cabin to get some food for their new friend, who they called Roscoe. Chase was brought from the cabin and introduced to the fox. They became unlikely friends. But still a bit wary, whenever Roscoe visited the cabin, he kept his distance from Chase.

Trapping season would be starting soon and the couple had not yet taken a full inventory of the fur shed and organized it and the storage area to their liking. They were planning on doing this job today. Johnathan's cabin was a jewel in this piece of paradise. The previous resident of the cabin was meticulous and had arranged every item, each having its own place. This left the couple with very little work to do, other than ensuring they had everything needed for the season.

Finishing in the fur shed, the couple took Chase and left him in the cabin. Shining Star retrieved her net, as she was taking Johnathan fishing. The couple launched the canoe into the lake and thirty minutes later they had caught enough fish for dinner. Having extra time, Johnathan had an idea. They would paddle the canoe to the beaver dam. If they saw one of these cautious mammals, they would shoot it for additional food. As a bonus, Shining Star could use the fur to make two beaver hats for them to wear this winter.

The canoe moved in silence across the lake. As the couple drew nearer to the beaver dam, Johnathan picked up his rifle while Shining Star continued to paddle. The atmosphere was silent as they approached the beaver house. Sudden movement in the water caught Johnathan's attention. A beaver's head rose above the water, unaware of the danger he was facing. Johnathan shot the beaver with his rifle, the loud discharge echoing across the lake. Shining Star paddled closer; they retrieved the dead animal and loaded into the canoe. The couple could not have had a better day.

CHAPTER FIFTY-ONE

Johnathan and Shining Star paddled back with the fish Shining Star had caught with her net and the beaver in the bottom of the canoe. After a brief trip, the couple found themselves back at their cabin. The couple took the beaver to the fur shed, where Shining Star taught Johnathan how to skin the beaver for its pelt. Then Shining Star butchered the animal for food, with Johnathan watching how she cut the meat from the carcass. Three hours later, the beaver hide was stretched and drying, and the fish Shining Star caught were cleaned and ready to eat for dinner.

Johnathan took the fish remains and put them in the lake. These inedible parts of the fish would become food for turtles and other hungry scavengers looking for an easy meal. The remains of the beaver would be used later to bait a trap to try to catch the wolverine, who had made his presence known at the cabin at least a dozen times looking for food. Johnathan returned to the cabin. The column of smoke rising from the chimney meant Shining Star had started a fire. The crackling of the wood meant the stove was hot enough to boil water.

Shining Star planned to cook a delicious stew from

the meat of the beaver. A light scratching at the cabin door caught Johnathan's attention. It was Roscoe, who had smelled the meat and fish and was looking for a handout to satisfy his hunger. Shining Star had saved the hungry fox some meat from the butchered beaver, which the canine most graciously accepted. Shining Star got the meat on the stove, then left the cabin to gather plants she needed to add to the pot to make the stew. She returned after a brief time, adding them to the already cooking meat.

Johnathan and Shining Star decided to rest while the stew was cooking. They added wood to the stove and then laid down in their bed. After a playtime of kissing, hugging, and tickling, the couple fell asleep. Shining Star dreamed about her father. In her dream he was an eagle, flying majestically across the sky, watching over the earth. Shining Star knew her father's spirit would protect Johnathan and her from harm.

The couple were abruptly wakened by the sound of a dog barking outside the cabin. Getting out of bed to investigate, Chase was already at the cabin door, ready to see what was going. The sound of voices outside surprised the couple. Looking out the window, a smile spread across Shining Star's face. It was her cousin, Wendy, her husband, Jason, and their one-year-old child, who Wendy was carrying on her back. The couple and their baby were invited into the cabin, while the dogs were left outside and soon became friends.

CHAPTER FIFTY-TWO

After happy greetings and hugs, Shining Star offered the couple a bowl of the beaver stew, which was on the stove and ready to eat. They sat at the table after feeding the dogs the rest of the raw beaver meat, which Shining Star had put away. The year-old baby sat on Wendy's lap, sharing food with his mother. Jason and Wendy were on their way to Dawson City to pick up Omar, their donkey, who had been staying at Bev's. The couple were going to use his services to pack in supplies to their cabin before the winter weather arrived. Johnathan and Shining Star knew they would soon have to do the same thing, using Honey as their pack animal. After the meal was finished, Jason and Wendy left, continuing their journey to Dawson. A quiet atmosphere followed, as their company left the cabin.

Johnathan and Shining Star's attention now turned to the wolverine. They had to do something to prevent this animal from wreaking havoc on their trap line this winter. Shining Star had a plan; she shared with Johnathan how the Indigenous people catch wolverines. They hang a snare, covered with rancid bait from a tree branch, attached to a higher limb. For the wolverine to retrieve the meat, it must jump up for it. When the animal attempted and grabbed his prize, he would get caught in the suspended snare.

Shining Star told Johnathan that sometimes this method caught the wolverine but usually did not kill it. She thought if they hung a steel trap from a tree, it would cause the animal's death, rather than just disabling it. Wolverines have been known to chew their leg or arm off to escape a steel-jawed trap when caught in one on the trapline. The couple did not want to risk the animal escaping, which is why suspending the trap was a good idea.

Johnathan retrieved a leg trap from the fur shed and together they baited it and attached a longer chain for anchoring it in a higher tree branch. The couple set off into the bush to scout for a place to set their trap. As they entered the bush, a perfect location immediately came into view, a tree which Johnathan could easily climb with strong branches to hold the trap. In virtually no time, the job was finished, and the couple stood back and observed their handiwork. The trap was set, and it looked like it would catch the elusive wolverine.

The couple returned to the cabin and Shining Star suggested they dig out the pool at the bottom of the freshwater spring. Over the summer it had filled with sand and if not cleaned out the water will freeze during the harsh winter months. Shining Star suggested they bring the gold pans and sift through the sand they remove from the pool. The couple gathered up the gold pans and shovel and after a short walk, they reached the spring. Johnathan walked to the water and dug shovels of sand from the shallow pool, placing the sand in a clearing a short distance from the spring.

Shining Star, who was watching Johnathan, caught a flash of gold in the sand. She told Johnathan to stop digging for a minute. She reached down and sifted through the last shovel of sand he had dumped on the ground. Her heart skipped a beat as her hands grasped what felt like a small rock. It was a gold nugget, which Johnathan estimated to weigh a half an ounce. It was larger than any nugget he had found while prospecting for gold in California.

Excited, Johnathan finished digging the sand from the pool and together the couple panned the sand piles. They found three more nuggets, which were smaller in size than the first one but were still larger than the average size found by prospectors in the area. They also uncovered a knife, which was likely dropped in the pool by mistake when someone collected water from the spring. The couple gathered up their tools and treasures and returned to the cabin surprised at the outcome of their brief trip.

CHAPTER FIFTY-THREE

The month of September would soon be coming to an end. Johnathan could not let any more time slip by before leaving to go get the necessary supplies to help the couple navigate through the winter more comfortably. Johnathan was buying a heavy blanket for their bed, as well as extra coffee, sugar and flour, if they were available. All these goods would be carried by Honey, who would accompany them back to the cabin one last time before winter arrived.

It was a cold cloudy morning when the trio left the cabin for Dawson. They had little food to take with them, only a meager supply of smoked fish. The day passed by quickly and the group soon found themselves at the halfway point of their journey. The lake was dark like the sky, an uninviting expanse of water stretching before the couple's eyes. Johnathan collected boughs from nearby evergreen trees to lay on the cold ground for their bed. The couple started a fire to keep warm; the nights getting cold for sleeping outside under the stars. The trio shared the remainder of their food, which did not satisfy their appetites.

With no shelter, the couple's sleep was uncomfortable. Daybreak and the promise of sunshine lifted their spirits as the morning sun rose over the horizon. The small group broke camp and were expecting to arrive at their destination by early afternoon. The day was sunny but cold, with a frigid wind blowing from the north. The weather was a reminder to the couple winter would soon be approaching. After a tiring day of walking for Johnathan and Shining Star, the buildings in Dawson were a pleasant sight to see. It meant an end to their journey, a warm bed to sleep in, and good food to eat.

The trio walked to the hotel, where they stayed while in Dawson. The innkeeper greeted them with a big smile and a hearty "Welcome back!". He told the couple roast beef and potatoes were on the menu for dinner tonight in the dining room. The trio retired upstairs to their assigned room, where the couple washed up in the large wash basin which sat in the corner by the window. Without hesitation, they then collapsed on the bed and fell asleep. The first call for dinner from downstairs awakened them a couple of hours later. With Chase in tow, the group walked downstairs to the dining room to eat.

The overpowering aroma of roast beef cooking greeted their senses as they entered the dining area. The dinner was excellent, the couple eating two large portions of roast beef and potatoes. Chase also ate dinner, a dish the innkeeper's wife made specifically for dogs. After finishing the meal with apple pie for dessert, Johnathan, Shining Star, and Chase returned to their room, their stomachs full. The couple immediately fell into bed, where they slept peacefully till the following morning. The pleasantries of their dreams reflected the young couple's happy lives living in the Yukon. What most people called hell, they viewed as paradise.

CHAPTER FIFTY-FOUR

When Johnathan and Shining Star woke the following morning, they were well rested. The couple rose from their bed early, knowing they had numerous chores to do today. Johnathan wanted to go to Bev's house first, to let her know they were in town and they would be removing Honey from her care for a short while. Bev, happy to see the young couple, invited them for dinner and to stay overnight. She suggested it would be easier for them to leave for their cabin from her house. Bev also told Shining Star she would love their company for the evening, so the couple agreed to Bev's hospitable offer.

Honey, on the other hand, was not pleased to see Johnathan and Shining Star. She knew what their presence meant, a trip into the dangerous forest with her back ladened down with heavy goods and predators hiding in the woods waiting to eat her. Honey hated the job Johnathan expected her to do and would prefer to stay at Bev's, waiting for Omar to return. Here she knew she was safe and would never go hungry. However, Honey was taken from her safe habitat and put to work.

The couple led the donkey around town, visiting different businesses until Johnathan and Shining Star had gathered everything on their list. Honey's cooperative behaviour today earned her a special treat from the livery stable, a mixture of a donkey's favorite grains, a special mash made up by the proprietor of the business himself. After Honey ate her tasty snack, the group returned to Bev's house, their work done. Johnathan took his donkey to the barn where her back was unloaded for the evening. Shining Star would repack the goods Honey would carry to the cabin in the morning.

Bev had a venison stew, ladened down with real vegetables, cooking on the stove for dinner. Root vegetables such as carrots, turnips, and beets are grown in the Yukon during the short growing season and are available for a brief period during the late fall. The meals Bev prepared were always delicious. Her fresh baked bread melted in one's mouth and her foods were always cooked to perfection; tonight's dinner was no exception.

During dinner, Bev invited Johnathan and Shining Star to her house for Christmas. Jason and Wendy were attending with their baby, as well as Steward, Wendy's brother. He would never miss the Christmas celebration at Bev's, as she was his favorite aunt. It was past midnight when goodnights were exchanged among the tired host and her guests. Chase laid down by the woodstove, while Johnathan and Shining Star retired to the second bedroom upstairs. Leaving for their cabin tomorrow was fresh in the young couple's minds as they drifted off to sleep.

CHAPTER FIFTY-FIVE

The smell of frying meat greeted the couple's senses upon awakening. Bev was cooking breakfast, making sure Johnathan and Shining Star had a full stomach before leaving on their return trip to their cabin. Chase had already eaten his breakfast, as he was always in the front of the line wanting to be the first one to be fed. Bev also packed two moose bones for Chase to take home with him. Huskies love to chew on the bones until they get to the marrow inside. To this breed of dog, the bone marrow from the moose is a delicacy rarely available to enjoy.

After a pleasant conversation and a tasty breakfast, the couple said their goodbyes to Bev. They placed the goods they purchased in Dawson on Honey's back, leaving Bev's home for their journey back to the cabin. The last flocks of Canadian geese migrating south flew overhead, filling the air with their song. The group walked all day, finally reaching the halfway point of their journey by nightfall. The light of the full moon shone down on Johnathan and Shining Star while they prepared their campsite. Johnathan started a fire with wood left over from a previous visit here. The nights were getting colder, as Mother Nature was changing the season to late fall. Soon the fire was hot, the crackling wood sending a cloud of wispy smoke skyward. The group of travellers slept soundly. The quiet of the forest was only interrupted occasionally by the wind, a strong breeze blowing through the limbs of the naked trees, whose leaves were lying on the forest floor.

At first light Johnathan and Shining Star were awakened by Chase's barking. A squirrel gathering crumbs of leftover food was voicing its displeasure at the dog who disrupted his breakfast and chased him up a tree. The couple awake, pulled themselves up from the cold ground and prepared to leave. They hoped to pick up their pace of travel and arrive at the cabin before nightfall. The day was warm with a light breeze from the south, a warm wind rarely felt this far north in the late fall.

The sun was setting as the cabin came into view. Johnathan removed the goods from Honey's back and locked her in her enclosure where she would be safe. Shining Star entered the cabin to start a fire in the woodstove, glad to be home. Johnathan placed the supplies the couple purchased in Dawson in the storage area in the fur shed. After finishing this job, he joined Shining Star inside the cabin for dinner.

The couple ate smoked venison and moose meat for dinner, which Bev had packed for them before they left Dawson. Chase enjoyed chewing on one of the moose bones she had included in the pack for him. Bev was an elder in her tribe and was often gifted meat from large game animals, such as moose and bear. Indigenous hunting parties shot these animals to help feed their people. Bev's house was a place for the local natives to pick up bones for their dogs and in the winter frozen meat for stews and soups. The hunting parties would bring the meat to Bev's place and from here it would be distributed to the native people living in the Dawson area.

Everyone in Johnathan's traveling party went to bed with a full stomach, including Honey, who ate the special mash the proprietor of the livery stable in Dawson had made. Johnathan had bought as much of his donkey's favorite food as he thought he could comfortably carry home before leaving Dawson. The forest was quiet as fatigue overwhelmed the weary travellers. Tomorrow morning Johnathan would take Chase and check the trap they had set to catch the wolverine. Johnathan's hope was to find a dead wolverine hanging in the tree, the end of his annoying problem.

CHAPTER FIFTY-SIX

The spirit of the north draws a breed of man who's only hope is to survive in this land with nature; the will to survive in a place which shows no mercy, only death to the unprepared. These men, their last thoughts as they died in the wilderness were just a memory taken to their death, never to be erased from their conscience.

The birds were singing, filling the cabin with song. Chase was awake, waiting to be let outside. Shining Star rolled over in bed, clearly indicating to Johnathan what her intentions were, she wanted to be left to sleep. Johnathan rolled out of bed and got dressed. The air outside was warm, so there was no need for a jacket. He said goodbye to his wife, grabbed his rifle and left the cabin. Johnathan called the dog, who was playing with Roscoe, now Chase's friend. The young fox never left the area of the cabin, feeling safe with the new family he had adopted.

Johnathan and his dog started walking toward the location where they had set the trap for the wolverine. Hanging from the trap was a wolverine's leg. He had chewed it off to escape the trap. Instead of jumping up for the bait, the animal must have climbed the tree, attempting to retrieve the meat from above. The trap was set off by the wolverine after he climbed onto it, resulting in the animal's leg getting caught in it. His only option to break free was chewing off his own leg, allowing him to escape back into the forest.

Johnathan returned to the cabin and told Shining Star what happened. She told Johnathan the wolverine's leg would heal, and he would now be very wary, mad, and difficult to find. The wolverine would never show its face around the cabin again but would watch Johnathan from the forest. He would never expose himself to what he perceived as danger. The animal knew who was responsible for him losing his leg and he was vindictive. The wolverine had a plan, to kill Johnathan's pack animal. He would find a way into her shelter and rip her throat out, leaving her to bleed to death on the floor of her stall. The wolverine knew this would bring Johnathan great distress, and he would cherish this revenge.

Shining Star told Johnathan the animal would stay quiet until the site of his amputation healed enough to allow free movement again. Hearing this, Johnathan decided to take his rifle and his dog and go hunting for the wounded wolverine. Three hours later, Johnathan returned to the cabin telling Shining Star he had not seen any sign of the animal.

In the late afternoon, Jason and Wendy unexpectedly dropped in. They had Omar with them as they were returning to Dawson to drop him off at Bev's, where he would be boarded for the winter. Wendy gave Shining Star some venison Jason had shot the day before. An invitation to spend the night was extended to the couple by Johnathan, which they gratefully accepted. It would be an evening which would change the course of someone's life in Johnathan's family forever.

CHAPTER FIFTY-SEVEN

It was nearing mid October in the Yukon and winter would soon be here. The lake which sat in front of Johnathan's cabin was quiet, as the migratory waterfowl had left before freeze-up, flying to warmer climates down south. The two young couples relaxed in the cabin, sharing stories about their experiences in the Yukon. Both couples were happy for the life they had built here.

The north wind blew hard, rattling the windows of the cabin. The fire in the woodstove created a warmth which radiated throughout the space. Shining Star mentioned to Wendy that they had to return Honey back to Dawson, as she would also be wintering over at Bev's. Jason suggested they take Honey with them. She could keep Omar company on the journey, and this would save Johnathan and Shining Star a trip to Dawson. This gesture proved having friends while living in the wilderness was beneficial, a little kindness goes a long way in the north.

Jason and Wendy's dog, King, had accompanied them on their trip and was now outside with Chase. This is where both animals would sleep tonight due to a lack of space inside the cabin. The wolverine watched the cabin from a safe distance. He was aware of Omar's presence, as he had followed the group here after picking up the donkey's scent in the forest. The wolverine had not decided when he was going to make his move but knew he would wait until Omar left. He was focused on carrying out his original plan of attacking and killing Honey.

It was approaching midnight when the occupants of the cabin retired to bed. John, Wendy, and their son, Kuzih, would be leaving in the early morning on their trip to Dawson, with both Omar and Honey. The couple told Johnathan and Shining Star they would stop in on their return trip and take them to their cabin. From this location it was a short distance to where Wendy's brother lived. Wendy had arranged for them to purchase a couple of dogs from Steward and would take them to his property to look at them. Steward was in the business of breeding and raising huskies and had sold many healthy sled dogs to area residents, including men from Dawson.

As the winter solstice drew nearer, the sun rose later in the morning each day. Jason and Wendy drank coffee and ate some smoked meat for breakfast along with their hosts. They gathered up the animals and by 9 a.m., said farewell, disappearing into the forest. Watching from a distance, the wolverine realized his diabolical plan had been foiled. Honey was gone and he had no idea if she would ever return. Disappointed, the wolverine slunk back off into the forest hoping for a better day.

CHAPTER FIFTY-EIGHT

Almost a week went by before Jason and Wendy returned to Johnathan and Shining Star's cabin. Wendy said the trip to Dawson had turned into quite a spectacle. Wendy explained to the listening couple she was in front of the group carrying her baby, while Jason was next in line leading Honey, with Omar at the rear. The forest was quiet, the trip to Dawson being monotonous. It was a long journey on a tough trail through the unforgiving wilderness of the Canadian north. Travellers on this route anticipate an occasional wolf or bear attack but Jason and Wendy never imagined what happened on their trip to town.

As Jason slowly led Honey down the trail, the tranquility was shattered by what sounded like a victory cry coming from Omar. This was followed by a scream emanating from Honey. Startled, Jason and Wendy stopped and stared, not believing their eyes. Omar had mounted Honey and was breeding her. The couple looked on in shock and disbelief. Honey had given Jason and Wendy no clues she was in heat.

Jason jumped into action, wanting to prevent a pregnancy. He positioned himself behind Omar and tried to pull him off Honey. This reaction was to no avail, as Omar was holding on tight and not about to let go. Jason gave up, letting Omar finish his commitment to the procreation of his species. Wendy told Shining Star when they left Bev's house for the trip home, the two love birds were together in the barn with the wife likely pregnant. A roar of laughter came from the two couples at the conclusion of the story. Their friendship had been cemented further by the actions of their two donkeys.

Jason and Wendy had returned with coffee and jerky for Johnathan and Shining Star. Johnathan had requested the couple pick up these favorite commodities while in Dawson if they were available. Shining Star asked Jason and Wendy to join them for dinner, as she had an abundant supply of fish. She had stored fresh filets in the outside freezer, which was now usable as the weather had turned colder. In a couple of weeks, this storage area would be cold enough to keep moose and deer meat for the winter.

After dinner, a pleasant conversation ensued as the two couples became better friends. Tomorrow, after breakfast, they would travel together to Jason and Wendy's cabin. It was a trip Johnathan and Shining Star were looking forward to. It would be their first trip to see another wilderness cabin like their own, a welcome distraction in the lives of this busy couple.

CHAPTER FIFTY-NINE

The moon shone brightly, bathing Johnathan's cabin in light. The howl of a lone wolf reverberated through the dark forest, waking Shining Star from her sleep. She listened to the wolf's message, which was a soulful search for her dead mate, who had died at the hands of a trapper and his rifle earlier that day. A chance encounter between man and wolf had taken the life of this majestic predator of the North. The wolf felt alone, her soul empty from the loss of her mate, her mournful howl reflecting this moment.

The two couples slept peacefully inside the cabin. At one point, Johnathan woke from his sleep and felt the cabin was cold. He got up from bed and added more wood to the fire and within a short time, the cold air was replaced by warmth, as the woodstove performed it's magic. Johnathan returned to bed with Shining Star. The couple's love for one another had blossomed. He wrapped his arms around his wife and in a brief time he was back asleep.

Johnathan had placed Chase and King in Honey's empty enclosure for the night. He did not want the dogs to have an encounter with the wolverine, who was still active in the area. An unwanted meeting with this animal could result in an attack and death for one of the dogs.

The wolverine was on the roof of the cabin, having adapted well to life with three legs. The amputation of his leg did not hamper the wolverine's ability to move around or climb. He knew where the dogs were and would look to pick a fight with them if given the chance. The wolverine looked around at the surrounding forest, which was bathed in moonlight. Observing movement in the trees, he exited the roof to investigate a possible food source in the forest.

The morning sun cast its light over the cabin. Jason and Wendy's baby was crying, wishing to be fed. Johnathan got out of bed and dressed. He went outside and let Chase and King out of their secured enclosure. He fed the dogs from the outside freezer and then returned to the cabin. Jason and Wendy were awake, taking care of Kuzih. Shining Star was stoking the fire in the woodstove, wanting to heat water to make coffee for her company, Johnathan, and herself.

The four adults ate breakfast together. Afterwards they gathered their belongings, securing the door when they left. Jason told Shining Star it was a four hour walk to their cabin. With luck, the group would arrive there shortly after lunch. The day had turned cloudy and cold, with a hint of snow in the air. After what seemed like a short time, they reached their destination, Jason and Wendy's home.

CHAPTER SIXTY

King was the one in the group who was happiest to be home. He ran around the cabin sniffing for new scents left by animals visiting here while they were on their trip to Dawson. The first thing Johnathan and Shining Star noticed about the cabin was its size, it was twice the size of their cabin. Jason and Wendy had added on to the original building to create more living space when the baby was born.

Jason and Wendy had an established homestead. Wendy had a garden behind the cabin, where she grew root vegetables. This ensured they would have vegetables, such as carrots and turnips, for her stews until Christmas. Jason showed the couple his fur shed and the attached area he used for storing his sled and harnesses for the dogs. Jason took two dogs from Steward for the winter, returning the animals to him in the spring. Johnathan and Shining Star were hoping to set up the same arrangement with Steward.

Jason had purchased enough wood to assemble two dog houses for the dogs to stay in during the winter while at his cabin. He showed Johnathan the shelters for the dogs, explaining he had picked up the lumber from Steward. A friend of Steward's, who lived a short distance away, had built a workable sawmill which utilized waterpower. Steward had purchased the wood from this entrepreneur, who had managed to establish a good business in the wilderness. Johnathan thought supplying dog houses for his dogs was not an issue because he planned to house them in the barn where Honey had formerly been sheltered.

Jason and Wendy's cabin sat on a beautiful lake which provided a variety of food for the couple. Jason said the loons' song provided comfort during the summer months and their disappearance in the fall to head for warmer climates signaled the onset of winter. The birds had left the lake weeks earlier. Jason and Johnathan took the canoe and went fishing. The skies had cleared, and the sun was out, shining its warm rays down on the men in the canoe. With hook and line, they caught enough fish for dinner. The fish would be cleaned and prepared outside over a fire tonight.

The men returned to the cabin, happy with their luck at being able to provide fresh food to eat. Wendy had purchased flour and the other ingredients needed to bake bread and was putting a loaf in the oven of her woodstove. It would be a delicious compliment to the fish for dinner. The day passed and night fell in the forest surrounding Jason and Wendy's cabin.

Shining Star lit the campfire and the couples sat around it conversing freely while they waited for the fire to get hot. Shooting stars filled the sky. It was a meteor shower, something the couples had not seen before. The night ended early, as the cold night air became uncomfortable. Everyone retreated into the cabin where they spent the rest of the evening talking. The couples were enjoying the company they were providing to one another, an uncommon event in this land called the Yukon.

CHAPTER SIXTY-ONE

Johnathan looked out the cabin window and saw the dawn sky was filled with dark storm clouds. Snowflakes filled the air; like balls of white cotton, they fell from the sky aimlessly floating to the ground, melting upon impact. This show of winter ended, the taste of what was to come was over. Mother Nature's warning would soon be a reality for the people who lived in this wilderness. With the advent of winter, survival would become man's top priority in this unforgiving land.

Today's plan was to walk to Steward's cabin. Johnathan and Shining Star were going to select two strong dogs to help Chase pull the sled used for servicing their trapline this winter. The team and sled would also be used on their trip to Dawson City at Christmas. The group ate breakfast and prepared to leave for Wendy's brother's house, which was a two hour walk away from Jason and Wendy's cabin.

The couples left for Steward's with Chase and King in tow. It was a cold day, but the skies had cleared allowing the sun to shine down on the travellers. After what seemed like a short walk, Steward's cabin came into view. Wood smoke spewed out of the chimney, a welcoming sign of a warm place to get out of the uncomfortable cold of late fall. Steward welcomed his sister Wendy, his cousin Shining Star, and their husbands into his cabin. Chase and King were also welcomed inside, their presence around Steward's dogs had set off a chorus of loud barking and snarling from the animals that would not stop.

Steward offered everyone a piece of smoked fish and some hot tea. He was continually catching fish from the lake his cabin sat on, which provided Steward with an endless supply of food for himself and his dogs. After socializing for an hour, Steward was ready to let Johnathan and Shining Star pick out two dogs from him. He showed them two sisters from the same litter, which were a year old. Johnathan and Shining Star happily accepted the two dogs into their family, calling them Ginger and Shirley.

The couple made a deal with Steward like the one Jason and Wendy had with him. The dogs would stay with them for the winter and return to Steward in the late spring. He would house them, providing exercise and care in the warmer months. When the snow arrived, Steward would deliver the dogs to Johnathan and Shining Star's cabin.

Having settled all the details about the dogs with Steward, the visitors said goodbye and returned to Jason and Wendy's cabin. Johnathan and Shining Star would spend one more night there and return home tomorrow, the proud owners of two new dogs, Ginger and Shirley. The couple couldn't wait for mid-November when the huskies would arrive at their new home. They were sure the dogs would prove to be a fine addition to their growing family.

CHAPTER SIXTY-TWO

The following morning came quickly. It was time for Johnathan and Shining Star to leave Jason and Wendy's cabin and return home. They thanked the couple for their help and hospitality and promised to return in early December. Johnathan and Shining Star's new dog team would have to learn to mush together in the snow before they would visit again. Jason and Wendy followed their friends out the door to say goodbye, their eyes following the couple and Chase down the trail until they were out of sight. Jason and Wendy returned inside, their sleeping baby would waken soon and want to be fed.

The day was sunny but cold, with a strong north wind blowing against Johnathan and Shining Star's backs as they made the journey home. Chase, always looking for an adventure, spent his time on the trail chasing squirrels up trees. Once successful, he would then sit at the base of the tree and further aggravate the rodents by barking. The squirrels would respond to Chase with a chatter of abuse, which the couple were glad they could not understand.

After a long, uneventful walk, Johnathan and Shining Star's cabin came into view. Chase ran on ahead of the group to investigate. The couple were glad to be home and looked forward to sleeping in their own bed tonight. Dampness and a musty smell greeted the pair as they entered their home. Shining Star immediately lit a fire in the stove and before long heat was spreading through the building, making it cozy and comfortable again.

The north wind was blowing hard across the lake, causing a loose board on Honey's enclosure to bang loudly. Shining Star's intuition told her the first blizzard of the season was on its way. Preparations had to be made at the prospect of a long-lasting storm with high winds and blowing snow. The couple carried in a three-day supply of fuel for the woodstove from outside the cabin. Johnathan collected extra water from the freshwater spring and the lake. Shining Star secured any loose items around the property and retrieved the remaining fish from the outdoor freezer.

The winds blew hard throughout the night, keeping the couple awake. At daybreak, the Yukon's first major snowstorm of the winter season unleashed its fury on the simple lives of Johnathan and Shining Star. The snow and blowing wind kept the couple confined to their cabin for twenty-four hours. Once the storm had passed, eighteen inches of snow was on the ground. This was a substantial amount of precipitation for so early in the winter season.

Chase loved his new playground, running and jumping into the snowdrifts, burying his head under the snow. He was in his element, as huskies love living in the snow and cold. When threatened by a blizzard with no shelter, these dogs will lay down and let the snow cover them, creating an insulating blanket over them. After the storm passes, the husky stands up, shakes the snow off himself, and continues what it was doing. If humans could act this way, life would be easier and survival much simpler.

CHAPTER SIXTY-THREE

The following morning Johnathan and Shining Star donned snowshoes and went hunting for small game. Rabbits and grouse were plentiful in the forest surrounding their property. The couple left the cabin with Chase accompanying them, as they stayed on the trail used for the trapline. The bright sunshine reflected off the white snow creating an illusion of shiny sparkling stars spread across the landscape.

Chase, who had run ahead of Johnathan and Shining Star, had stopped and seemed interested in the tracks he found. Barking, he waited for Johnathan to catch up to him. Upon inspection, Johnathan understood Chase's interest; it was the wolverine. The tracks indicated the animal had three legs instead of four. The wolverine tracks crossed the trail where Chase was sniffing. The tracks in the snow were fresh, so Johnathan and Shining Star decided to follow the wolverine's trail into the forest. The couple hoped it would lead to the wolverine's den. After attempting to follow the tracks through the thick brush, Johnathan felt they were getting nowhere close to their goal of sighting the animal. Shining Star agreed, as they abandoned their search for this elusive northern predator and continued hunting.

Over the next two hours, the couple shot two rabbits and three grouse. The breast meat of this bird was a delicacy when prepared properly. Some old trappers swear it's the best tasting meat harvested from the bush. The group returned to the cabin, refreshed from the walk and happy their hunt was successful.

A surprise awaited the couple upon their return, Steward was sitting on a sled in their front yard, pulled by six dogs, including Ginger and Shirley. Johnathan and Shining Star were surprised to see Steward, as they had not been sure when to expect him. He unhooked Ginger and Shirley from the rest of the team and handed the two dogs over to Johnathan. Johnathan took the wary huskies and secured them in Honey's unused enclosure. This would be Ginger and Shirley's new home and shelter this winter.

Shining Star invited Steward into the cabin for coffee, which he felt obliged to do but would not stay long. His intuition told him another big storm was on its way. He did not want to be caught off guard at his cabin and be unprepared for a blizzard that could appear with no warning. After a short visit, Steward left for home. Johnathan and Shining Star watched as he mushed his dogs out of sight down the snow-covered trail.

The couple heeded Steward's advice and took watch over the weather. Dark menacing clouds filled the sky, but no snow fell from them. The snowstorm would arrive unexpectedly the next day. Respect for winter storms would be established after the couple endured a brief struggle with nature, a struggle they would be lucky to survive. Losing this battle would mean death in the fight for survival in this hostile land called Canada's north.

CHAPTER SIXTY-FOUR

The lake Johnathan and Shining Star's cabin sat on was not frozen over yet. The couple decided to take Shining Star's canoe and go fishing one more time before the lake became covered in ice. Once the lake started freezing over, they would need to stay off the forming ice until it was thick enough to hold their weight. This meant no fresh fish until the couple could start catching them from a hole they made through the ice.

The sky was dark and threatening but did not look like it was going to produce a storm, only passing snow showers. Johnathan and Shining Star launched their canoe into the frigid water of the lake. The couple paddled to a favoured area to fish with Shining Star's net. Over the next two hours they caught eight fish. When they returned to the cabin some of the meat would be smoked while the rest would be stored raw in the outside freezer.

The couple, in their quest to catch fish, had quit paying attention to the weather. A sudden strong wind blew the canoe sideways, catching Johnathan and Shining Star off guard. Snow started falling and the waves on the lake grew larger. With a sense of panic, the couple turned the canoe toward shore. Paddling into the waves caused water to splash into the canoe, soaking the passengers. A ten-minute canoe ride to shore turned into a trip which seemed to take forever. Shining Star prayed to her father to help them reach their cabin safely.

With a sense of relief, they reached the shoreline in front of the cabin and beached the canoe on the sand. Johnathan pulled the canoe out of the water and retrieved their fish. They walked briskly towards the cabin, frozen from the spray they received from the lake. Hypothermia would soon set in unless their bodies were warmed back up to a normal temperature.

Entering the warm cabin made the couple realize how close they came to dying on the lake. Going fishing in the canoe this late in the season was a risk the couple should have avoided. Johnathan and Shining Star stripped off their wet clothes and added wood to the fire. The couple were soon feeling better. They climbed into bed and pulled the warm blanket over their cold bodies. Within a brief time, the couple were sleeping, wrapped in each other's arms. Chase, who had been resting comfortably by the woodstove, paid no attention to what was going on between Johnathan and Shining Star.

The sound of dogs barking, and human voices abruptly woke everyone in the cabin, including Chase. Johnathan and Shining Star jumped out of bed and dressed just before a knock came to the cabin door. Johnathan looked out the window to identify the men. They were Northwest Mounted police from Dawson City. The couple knew the one constable, while the other man was new to the force and had just been stationed in Dawson.

Johnathan invited the two men into the cabin where they enjoyed coffee the officers had gifted them. They told Johnathan and Shining Star it was their first patrol of the winter using their dogsled. After their wellness check, the Mounties left, informing Shining Star they would be visiting Jason and Wendy's cabin next.

Snow drifted down from the grey winter sky, covering the trees of the forest in a cloak of white. Johnathan and Shining Star knew it was time to set their trapline and get ready for a season of adventure and survival. The couple would enjoy their first winter together in this land called the Yukon.

CHAPTER SIXTY-FIVE

Today was the day Johnathan's two new dogs, Ginger and Shirley, would be hooked up to the snow sled with Chase acting as lead dog. Shining Star, with her experience mushing dog sleds, took the lead in organizing this endeavour. Chase had been interacting with his female companions daily since their arrival from Steward's cabin and Ginger and Shirley had accepted him as the alpha male. They would respect and follow him when he was the lead dog, pulling the sled for work or play.

Shining Star hooked the excited huskies up to the sled and on her command the three dogs bolted forward almost throwing her off the sled. In their first group run, the three dogs proved they could work well together. Shining Star returned to the cabin and told Johnathan to join her on the sled. On Shining Star's command, the dogs bounded forward pulling tightly on their harnesses. The sled took off with ease across the snow, the weight of Johnathan's body was not an issue for these strong Yukon-born dogs to pull.

After the trial run, the animals were each given a moose bone as a reward for their good behaviour. This surprise for the dogs was compliments of the constables who had recently dropped in for a visit. Coffee for the humans and moose bones for the dogs were the gifts the law officers left for the occupants living in the wilderness.

Johnathan and Shining Star were pleased with the results from their dogs. A good dog team would ensure a successful trapping season. Ginger and Shirley were returned to their enclosure, while Chase followed Johnathan and Shining Star to the storage area where the animal traps were stored. The couple organized the traps, which were all steel-jawed leg traps of various dimensions. The sizes were different depending on the animal the trapper was trying to catch. Smaller traps were used to catch fishers and martens, smaller fur-bearing mammals, while larger traps were used to catch beavers and bobcats. The couple would set a dozen traps tomorrow, using the remains of the fish and the rabbit they shot for bait.

Planning to start their day early tomorrow, Johnathan and Shining Star returned to their cabin. The couple were excited at the prospect of starting their trapping season, as was Chase. The forest was dark and silent. Staring out the cabin window, Johnathan could make out the shape of large snowflakes drifting downward from the sky. Tranquility spread over the cabin as the young couple drifted off into a peaceful sleep, not awakening till the early dawn of the following morning.

CHAPTER SIXTY-SIX

The constant chatter of a raven on the roof of the cabin was annoying Johnathan and Shining Star. The raven was watching Roscoe, the domesticated fox which resided at the cabin, eat the remains of a rabbit which had been killed by a raptor. Roscoe had dragged the carcass from the lake back to the cabin and was eating it for breakfast. The raven wanted Roscoe to share his food, but the fox paid no attention to his demands.

Johnathan pulled himself out of bed and got dressed. He let Chase outside and shooed the raven away. Roscoe, upon seeing Chase, grabbed the remains of his rabbit and ran to his den. Before the ground had frozen, the fox had dug himself a den under the cabin. This home provided him shelter from bad weather and a place to escape his enemies.

The day was sunny and cold, but the wind was calm with only a light breeze blowing through the forest. The couple gathered Ginger and Shirley from their dog pound. The dogs seemed content staying in Honey's old apartment, as it was warmer and safer than staying outside in a shelter made from wood.

Shining Star taught Johnathan how to hook up the

harnesses for the dogs. She also reviewed the signals and commands the dogs understood, which they had previously practiced. Within a short time, and with some excellent guidance from his wife, Johnathan learned the skills he needed to become a good musher. With the dogs excited and ready to go, the couple loaded the traps onto the sled, along with the bait for the traps and some water for the dogs. Barking loudly, the dogs pulled on their harnesses, anxious to go.

Shining Star released the brake on the sled and told the dogs to go. Like racehorses out of the gate, they ran at a breakneck speed down the trapline trail to the first emergency shelter. Shining Star stopped them here for a brief rest and to turn around. Johnathan and Shining Star would begin placing traps here and work their way back towards the cabin. They would also set snares along the way to catch rabbits, which would provide both food for his dogs and bait for the traps. A deer hunt was also being planned to take place shortly, as a cache of meat in the outdoor freezer was needed to starve off hunger this winter.

Shining Star taught Johnathan where and how to set the different sized traps and tricks to use to increase their chances of catching fur-bearing mammals. She spent the day teaching Johnathan about trapping and how to set rabbit snares on the runways the rabbits used in the winter. When the snow is deep, snowshoe rabbits make trails through the forest called runways. They use these packed down paths through the landscape to move around with ease. Snares set on these runways are a sure death sentence for this animal, with strangulation in the cold snow the result.

With their work finished, Shining Star led the dogs home. The couple's first day of laying out the traps was a success. Reaching the cabin without incident, Johnathan unhooked the dogs from their harnesses and returned Ginger and Shirly to their shelter. He left the sled where it stood, as it would be used tomorrow to go hunting. Johnathan hoped venison or moose would soon be on their menu for dinner.

CHAPTER SIXTY-SEVEN

Johnathan woke up at daybreak to go hunting. His outdoor freezer was ready to be filled with meat. He was hoping to tag a deer or a moose today with Chase's help. The dog would pull the sled to the first emergency shelter, where Johnathan had seen deer sign yesterday. He could tell from the tracks in the snow there were at least four deer in the area. He would unhook Chase from the sled, and they would follow the deer tracks into the forest. Johnathan had a hunch the deer were sheltering in a stand of aspens not far from the shelter.

The day was gloomy, with a cloud filled sky when Johnathan and Chase left the cabin. Chase did well pulling the sled himself, as he was a strong, healthy dog. The pair soon reached the shelter and as expected, fresh deer prints littered the snow around the building. Johnathan unhooked Chase from the sled and the dog stayed close to Johnathan's side as the pair entered the wooded area behind the shelter. They followed the hoof prints in the snow for a short distance until they reached a large stand of aspen trees. Johnathan knew the deer would congregate here, as it was a food source and a good place to seek shelter from a storm.

Johnathan took up position behind an evergreen and

waited for one of the prized game animals to appear. Chase was impatient, wanting to run into the trees and flush the deer out where Johnathan could see them. Johnathan said no to Chase's idea. After a two hour wait, he detected movement on the edge of the treeline. A mature buck and three does came out from the trees, unaware of the danger they were facing.

Johnathan raised his rifle and without hesitation shot the buck in the head. The animal staggered backwards, Johnathan shooting again, hitting the deer in the leg. The male deer fell down dead, lying on the blood-stained snow. Johnathan told Chase he could go, and the dog immediately ran after the three deer who had escaped Johnathan's gun. A feeling of gratitude spread through Johnathan's soul after he shot this large animal. He thanked the spirits which provided him with this food; a mature buck produced almost the same amount of meat as two young does when butchered.

As Johnathan leaned over to examine his kill, a sudden ruckus from Chase snapped him back to the moment. The uproar was followed by the crashing sound of something running toward him. Chase had circled around behind the deer and was chasing them back toward Johnathan. Without hesitation, Johnathan raised his rifle and shot one of the deer. The animal died fifty feet from where the buck laid in the snow.

Johnathan decided to go back to the cabin and retrieve his wife and their other two dogs. The traps and snares would now have to wait to be checked tomorrow as harvesting the meat and transporting it back to the cabin was now the priority. Getting this work done before dark would be a challenge the couple and their dogs had to meet.

CHAPTER SIXTY-EIGHT

Johnathan left the deer where they died, took Chase and walked back to the sled. An hour later, they were pulling up to the cabin. The dog was unhooked from his harness and Johnathan entered the cabin with Chase following closely behind. Shining Star had boiling water on the woodstove and offered to make Johnathan coffee while he told the story about shooting the deer. He happily took her up on that offer.

Shining Star could not believe the luck Johnathan had. While he rested and drank his hot beverage, Shining Star retrieved Ginger and Shirley from their shelter. With Chase as lead dog, she hooked the huskies up to the sled. Johnathan stepped out of the cabin, walking to the tool area of the fur shed to retrieve another knife and a saw to cut bone. The couple's plan was to gut the animals where they died and then move them on the sled to the fur shed, where the meat would be processed.

Johnathan was able to maneuver the sled and dogs close to the kill site. The couple worked on the buck first. They gutted the animal and cut the bottom of the legs off the deer at the knee. Johnathan had hatched a plan.

They would load the whole carcass of the deer on the sled, draping it over the edges. Shining Star would be able to see over the body and mush the dogs while standing on the rear of the runners.

The couple successfully moved the dismembered carcass onto the sled. It was a perfect fit. Shining Star would take this load of meat home, pulling it off the sled close to the building where it would be butchered. She would then return to Johnathan's location to pick up the small doe, which also needed to be transported back to the cabin.

The wolverine, having heard the gunshots and now smelling the blood from the dead deer, drew close to the kill site. He watched Johnathan as he gutted the small doe. The wolverine was not the hunter he once was, as having only three legs was a handicap. The wolverine licked his lips, knowing he would be left with a buffet of leftover parts and pieces from the two deer after the couple left.

Shining Star returned with an empty sled. Johnathan loaded the carcass of the doe and with its weight, along with himself and Shining Star, the dogs strained to move the sled. Once back on the trail, the packed snow made the sled easier to pull. In a short time, the couple were back at the cabin with three panting dogs. Shining Star looked after the dogs while Johnathan pulled the deer carcasses into the shed. When the couple were done checking their trapline tomorrow, they would butcher the animals. Shining Star wanted to tan the hide of the buck and gift it to Bev for Christmas.

After finishing their chores, Johnathan and Shining Star returned to their cabin and added wood to the stove.

Warm air soon flooded the space, creating a peaceful and relaxing atmosphere for the couple. This was followed by sleep, which was not interrupted till daylight, the couple waking to face a busy day.

CHAPTER SIXTY-NINE

The first job a trapper living in the north woods does in the morning after he gets out of bed is feed and water his dogs. Dogs are always hungry and will eat anytime of the day or night. It is important to the trapper to take special care of his dogs, so he performed this task diligently every morning.

After taking care of his dogs, Johnathan woke Shining Star. They shared some venison cooked the night before and then got to work. The couple were taking the dogs to check the traps they had set two days before. Shining Star prepared the dogs and sled for travel, while Johnathan went to the fur shed and set up the tables for butchering the deer when the couple returned. Johnathan wanted to check the place where they had left the deer remains to see what animals had come last night to scavenge.

Excitement mounted as the dogs pulled the sled down the trail away from the cabin. Johnathan wondered which fur bearing mammal would be the first to be caught in one of their traps. The first three traps had been set for small mammals and were untouched. The fourth trap was larger, as Shining Star had noted multiple tracks in the area, which could have been made by a lynx. Lynx are large feline predators who prefer to eat small game, such as rabbits and squirrels, but also are scavengers. They will eat the remains of other animals they come upon in the forest while hunting.

As the dogs approached this location, they pulled harder on their harnesses and barked loudly. Johnathan, who was driving, brought the sled dogs to a stop and walked a short distance into the bush to check the trap. To his surprise, a lynx was caught, the animal's leg was firmly in the steel jaws of the trap which was not willing to let go. As Johnathan approached the trapped animal, the lynx growled and hissed aggressively. Knowing what he had to do, Johnathan raised his rifle and shot the animal in the head. Ruining this valuable pelt was not an option.

Johnathan retrieved his prize and proudly presented it to Shining Star, who was pleased with their first catch of the trapping season. Johnathan rebaited the trap and moved on. The rest of the trapline produced nothing but a half-eaten weasel, which had been left in the trap by a hungry raptor. This aerial predator had taken full advantage of the opportunity of a meal he did not have to work for.

Johnathan wanted to check one last thing before they headed back toward home, the activity at the deer remains left in the forest the evening before. Shining Star stayed with the dogs while Johnathan walked the short distance to the site. The first thing he noticed when he reached the scene were the tracks of the three-legged wolverine. Johnathan had expected to see evidence of this animal's presence, indicating he still lived in the area. Shining Star knew if they did not catch this animal, he would do his best to destroy their trapping season. The wolverine was now an enemy which needed to be exterminated.

CHAPTER SEVENTY

Johnathan returned to the sled, where Shining Star was waiting for him. She had turned the dogs around, heading them in the direction of the cabin. The couple were happy they had trapped a lynx, as it made them feel they were off to a good start. This endeavour they had chosen to embark on, fur trapping in a new frontier, could be challenging.

On the trip back to the cabin, Johnathan checked the snares he had set to catch rabbits. He found two large snowshoe hares, lying dead in the snow. He harvested the frozen bodies and placed them with the lynx on the sled. They continued their journey to the cabin, arriving without mishap. Johnathan unbuckled the dogs from their harnesses and returned Ginger and Shirley to their enclosure. After the deer was butchered, the dogs would be given the larger bones from the carcasses to chew on, a reward for their excellent work.

Johnathan and Shining Star ate a quick lunch and then turned their attention to butchering the deer Johnathan had shot. Johnathan worked on butchering the doe, while Shining Star began skinning the buck. She wanted to stretch and tan the hide to give to Bev as a gift for being her friend and aunt. The first step was to carefully remove the skin and then stretch it to begin the tanning process. Four hours later, their work was finished. Piles of fresh deer meat lay stacked on the table, which would be transferred later into the outside freezer. This storage area would keep their meat frozen until the spring. The inedible parts of the deer would also be stored there to be used as bait for the trapline.

Finished with their work for the day, Johnathan and Shining Star took the rest of the afternoon off. They enjoyed the heat which radiated off the hot black metal of the woodstove in the cabin and prepared venison steaks for dinner. Darkness comes early in this land of desolate forests and frozen lakes. The stillness during winter is captivating, the silence deafening to the senses. Shining Star told Johnathan it was the Spirit of the North. Shining Star's father had explained this to her when she was younger, but she had never experienced the true meaning of the message her father had been trying to convey until tonight. The couple shared this experience together as they continued their struggles with life in the Yukon.

CHAPTER SEVENTY-ONE

The howling north wind blew the snow up against the logs of the building. Roscoe felt safe in the den he had dug under the cabin. The fox had stockpiled some deer bones to chew on when inclement weather kept him below deck, which helped keep the fox from getting bored. Roscoe would dig out the snow from the entryway to his den when the wind died down and the snow quit blowing. To Roscoe this was like cleaning out his driveway.

The first rays of sunlight lit up the horizon. Johnathan and Shining Star stirred in their bed, waking from an uninterrupted sleep. The couple had set twelve additional traps yesterday beyond the first emergency shelter. Today they planned to set a dozen more, which would cover the entire trap line. This would take them to the emergency shelter at the end of the trail. From this location they would have access to several beaver colonies, making it a great choice to set some of the final traps on the trapline. The last shelter was also a good place to reorganize the sled before the couple headed back for home.

Shining Star put the dog team and snow sled together while Johnathan retrieved the traps and bait needed for the day. A brief time later, the sled left the cabin. The dogs' cloudy breath filled the air, like a steam locomotive travelling down a train track. Four hours later, the couple found themselves at the last shelter on the trail. Their haul of fur from the trapline was disappointing, only four small mammals had been caught. A few of the other traps had contained half-eaten and mutilated carcasses of animals. These crime scenes were surrounded by three-legged wolverine tracks. Johnathan knew it would have to be the end game for this animal who was costing them their livelihood. A serious discussion would be had over dinner between the couple about what had become a serious problem regarding the wolverine.

Before leaving the cabin this morning, Shining Star had retrieved two beaver traps and an axe from the shed. She wanted to show Johnathan how to set a trap to catch these elusive creatures. Along with the beavers' pelts being valuable, their meat was high in protein and popular in wilderness stews. Shining Star set two beaver traps, showing Johnathan how the Indigenous tribes set them. Good luck in catching these mammals could result in handsome rewards for the trapper.

It was well after noon when the couple finished at the beaver pond, meaning the sun would be setting before they arrived home. Johnathan didn't worry, as he recognized the dogs knew the trail and would take the couple back to the cabin safely after dark. Shortly after leaving the beaver dam, large flakes of snow began falling. When the dogs reached the shelter closest to the cabin, the group could go no further. Those innocent snowflakes they had encountered when leaving the far shelter had turned into a blizzard.

Johnathan sheltered the dogs as best he could and joined his wife in the shelter. She had started a fire in the fireplace using some of the dry wood stored for emergency stays. The couple took off their heavy coats and enjoyed the warm air coming from the fire. Shining Star had brought extra food with them, providing nourishment for her, Johnathan, and their dogs. The couple hoped the storm would end, enabling them to get back to their cabin tomorrow.

CHAPTER SEVENTY-TWO

At midnight, the blizzard ended with the moon shining its light over the cabin as the skies cleared. The night owl was calling, happy the storm was over. The couple slept peacefully, the fireplace keeping the shelter cozy and warm. The sun was shining down on the shelter when Johnathan and Shining Star got up. The couple had slept later than usual, only awakening when the dogs started barking.

Johnathan got dressed and went to feed the animals, while Shining Star gathered up their few belongings. They left the shelter for the forty-minute dogsled ride home, the dogs enthusiastic about getting back to the cabin, especially Chase. He felt like Johnathan and Shining Star were treating him more like a sled dog than a family pet. They had left him outside in the cold and snow all night with Ginger and Shirley, the sled dogs he worked with. Johnathan thought this experience would be good for Chase, as he wanted Chase to remain a strong-willed Yukon husky and not a dog who spent his life laying beside a warm fire. Chase did not agree with this new philosophy Johnathan had come up with, preferring his old way of life.

The dogsled arrived at the cabin without incident.

Johnathan locked Ginger and Shirley in their enclosure, letting Chase join the couple in the cabin. Later in the morning, Johnathan lit a fire in the woodstove of the fur shed. The couple wanted to thaw out the frozen pelts of the lynx and the rabbits, the animals they had previously retrieved from the trapline. They had been placed in the fur shed to protect the animals from any predators who would steal them. Shining Star wanted to work on the deer hide while Johnathan would work on removing the fur from the animals he had caught in the traps. Once Johnathan skinned an animal, Shining Star took possession of the hide to prepare it to sell in Dawson.

Twilight was approaching when Johnathan and Shining Star finished their work in the fur shed. The couple had cleaned the lynx and other fur-bearing animals, as well as the two rabbits they had snared. They were going to cook and eat the rabbits for dinner. The dogs would eat the last of their fresh supply of deer meat, all the rest having been placed in the freezer. Tomorrow the couple planned to go on the lake and cut some holes in the ice. Shining Star hoped to catch enough fish to feed the dogs and bait the traps using her net.

The couple had discussed the issue of the wolverine and decided to not set any more traps until he could be caught. Based on this species' reputation, they knew this would not be an easy task. Good luck would come their way regarding this problem. Perhaps it was an unrequested gift from Shining Star's father, who believed wolverines were evil. The Indigenous people accepted the killing of these animals, as the wolverine, a symbol of darkness in God's land, would never be missed.

CHAPTER SEVENTY-THREE

Johnathan looked out the cabin window at the snow blowing across the lake. In the early morning dawn, he watched as a deer ran out of the bush onto the frozen surface of the water, followed by a pack of wolves. Johnathan woke Shining Star to watch the wolf pack take down and kill the deer. He wondered if the wolves were new to this territory, as wolves had not been to the cabin since he shot two of the predators who tried to attack Honey. The six wolves easily caught up to the deer, who was floundering in the deep snow. The couple watched as the helpless animal was surrounded by the wolves. Without hesitation, the two lead wolves attacked and took the deer to its knees. The remaining wolves jumped in for the kill.

The wolves would eat their fill, leaving little for the scavengers to claim when they finished. The couple would take the dogs and travel to the kill site later. They were curious if the wolves would leave any of the deer they could use. Bait for their trapline or food for the dogs would be a good find. Nature's bounty can sometimes be shared by man.

Johnathan readied the dogs for the sled. They were

going to check the trapline and the two beaver traps they had set out on their last trip. The first six traps produced three pine martens, a woodland fur-bearing mammal with a small coat of fur. What Johnathan and Shining Star found at their seventh trap was shocking. The wolverine lay dead in the blood-soaked snow. The animal had chewed his other leg off to escape from the trap. Johnathan marveled at the animal's will to live. The wolverine had managed to make it three feet from the trap before collapsing in the snow. Unable to get back up, the wolverine had bled to death, the overwhelming trauma taking its life.

Johnathan retrieved the frozen body of the animal and placed it on the sled. Shining Star would tan the hide and they would take it to Dawson at Christmas. The fur would be given to the elders of Bev's tribe, where it would be displayed during sacred ceremonies. The presence of the wolverine pelt would remind the native people that danger always exists when this evil predator roams the forests of their sacred land.

The couple continued checking their trapline. Two ermine, small weasels whose fur turns white during the winter, were removed dead from the traps. The beaver traps were the last the couple checked. To their surprise, one of them held a fat male beaver. Johnathan pulled it up from under the ice, happily adding this prize to the bounty of animals on the sled. He rebaited the beaver trap and the couple left to return home.

A feeling of success overwhelmed the couple as they looked at all the fur sitting on the dogsled; it had been a successful start to the trapping season. The dog sled headed for the cabin with their wolverine problem solved. It was a horrible way for an animal known as a distinguished member of the forest to die. The picture of the wolverine's stubby front legs in the blood-soaked snow was a memory the couple would never forget, once again proving the brutality of this savage land.

CHAPTER SEVENTY-FOUR

The sled ride back to the cabin was uneventful, the packed snow on the trail making it easier to pull the heavy load on the sled. A surprise awaited the couple when they reached their destination, a team of barking sled dogs greeted them as they drew closer to their cabin. Smoke from the chimney curled skyward, making Johnathan hope whoever took over his cabin was a friend, not a foe. A man suddenly appeared in the doorway waving at the approaching sled. It was Steward, Wendy's brother.

Shining Star was pleased to see her cousin, who told the couple he was on his way to Dawson to sell some furs and pick up supplies. He had stopped for a visit and decided to wait in the cabin for their return. He hoped Johnathan didn't mind that he had started a fire in the woodstove to warm the home. Friendly greetings were exchanged, and Steward said he was surprised by all the fur on the couple's sled. He was especially curious about the dead wolverine with only two legs. Johnathan invited Steward to stay overnight. Happy to do so, Steward offered to help Johnathan process the furs they had brought home from their trap line.

The two men unloaded the dog sled, taking the dead

mammals into the fur shed to have their coats removed. A fire was started in the woodstove to heat the work area the men would be using. Shining Star brought out hot tea from the cabin for everyone. She oversaw the processing of the beaver, teaching Johnathan how to remove its pelt to get the best result. Shining Star then showed him how to butcher the beaver for its meat. She left the rest of the animal processing to the men, returning to the cabin to find something to feed their guest.

Three hours later, the work in the fur shed was finished and Johnathan and Steward returned to the cabin. The smell of venison frying on the woodstove caught their attention. The men were hungry, neither having eaten anything for a long time. The cabin felt warm and inviting and the smell of the food cooking on the stove whet their appetites. Fried venison was all the couple had to offer Steward, which was fine with him. He told Shining Star venison was his favorite meal, as the men sat to eat as soon as the food was ready.

The afternoon wore into evening. Shining Star talked to Steward about the Christmas party at Bev's house. Time was slipping by and soon the holiday would be here. Before the clock struck midnight, the people in the cabin were sleeping. The blowing snow on the lake covered the remains of the deer killed by the wolves. Not until the snow melts in the spring will the bones resurface, a reminder of the tragedy which befell this deer on that fateful day. Its life was a gift to the wolf pack who ate their fill.

CHAPTER SEVENTY-FIVE

The morning sun slowly rose above the horizon, its bright light promising the birth of another day. Steward rose from his bed on the floor and let Chase outside. The welcoming chorus of barking from his canine brothers woke Johnathan and Shining Star from their sleep. Steward ate smoked fish for breakfast, offering Johnathan and Shining Star some of the food he had carried with him from home. After a pleasant conversation over breakfast, Steward prepared to leave, promising to see his cousin and her husband at Bev's Christmas party. He thanked the couple for their hospitality, gathered his dog team and with loud barking from the huskies, said goodbye.

Silence returned to the cabin after Steward's departure. Johnathan and Shining Star prepared to leave the cabin themselves to check their trapline. The bright sunshine and cloudless sky prompted them to enjoy the outside environment. A warm front had arrived during the night, causing the snow to melt on the roof. This created a constant drip of water to fall from the eaves onto the melting snow below.

The couple's enthusiasm for the day waned as trap after

trap came up empty. Reaching the end of their trapline, they checked the beaver traps, with the same results. The couple decided to investigate this marshy area around the beaver dam more closely, looking for animal sign. They were pleasantly surprised to come across moose tracks.

Johnathan dreamed of shooting this moose and adding the meat to his outside freezer. When in Dawson at Christmas, he would organize a hunting party with Steward and Jason to take place in the new year. They would hunt together for the moose who was wintering in this area, and split the meat split three ways if they were successful. This would help the trappers feed themselves through the winter months when food was scarce and hard to find.

Johnathan followed the moose tracks out of the swamp into a wooded area. He stopped the dogs and asked Shining Star to wait for him. Walking into the bush, he disappeared but returned ten minutes later. He told Shining Star he had found the remains of a human body under a large fir tree, a man with a bullet hole through the skull. A gun was laying next to the body, pointing to a possible suicide. Johnathan had searched the man's pockets and found the remnants of a wanted poster, which he had seen before in Dawson. It depicted the cop killer from Edmonton, who was known to be in the area.

Johnathan left the remains where they lay and would report the body to the Mounties when they went to Dawson. He was certain this was the fugitive who had escaped the Mounties by running off into the forest. After days with no food or water, he probably became disorientated and lost, which eventually led to his suicide. The Mounties in

Dawson would be glad to clear this case, which they thought would never be solved.

The weeks went by, and the Christmas season was here. The couple retrieved all their traps from the bush and stored them in the emergency shelters until their return from town. Tomorrow morning Johnathan and Shining Star were leaving for Dawson, both looking forward to their Christmas celebration with Shining Star's family. This adventure would prove to be a nice break from the couple's difficult life in the bush.

CHAPTER SEVENTY-SIX

The dogsled was ready to be loaded for the couple's trip to Dawson. Earlier, during the morning sunrise, Johnathan had fed the dogs and readied them for this adventure. Like ships on an ocean, large white cumulus clouds moved through the blue sky. Shining Star thought it would be a beautiful day to travel by dogsled. Johnathan agreed with his wife, he was looking forward to the trip and the Christmas party at Bev's house.

Johnathan boarded up the cabin door, making it harder for wildlife intruders to enter the building while they were gone. The dogs were ready to go, pulling at their harnesses and barking loudly. Johnathan gave the dogs the signal to mush, and the huskies lurched forward. The dogsled moved easily through the snow. The morning on the trail was quiet, the only sounds in the forest were the panting of the dogs and the runners of the sled gliding over the snow.

At the halfway point to Dawson, Johnathan decided to stop the dogs and rest, giving his dogs water he carried on the sled. The sudden sound of canines barking broke the silence in the forest. A dog team was approaching, with two men at the helm and six dogs pulling the sled. It was the Northwest

Mounted Police from Dawson. As the men approached, the two parties recognized each other. A welcome greeting was exchanged between the Mounties and the fur trappers, the men telling Johnathan and Shining Star they were on a routine patrol they completed every year at this time. They were checking desolate cabins, finding some empty with no sign of the occupant.

Johnathan told the Mounties about finding the remains of a man in the forest. He gave the police the wanted poster he had found in the dead man's clothes and directions to the body. The Mounties were surprised and thankful for this information regarding this case, and promised the couple they would investigate their story. Johnathan also informed these men on patrol John, Wendy, and Steward would be in Dawson for Christmas and not at their cabins. Before continuing their respective travels, the Mounties gifted Johnathan and Shining Star some coffee, a gift to raise the spirits of the lonely men and women living deep in the wilderness of the Yukon.

The parties waved goodbye to one another, each dogsled heading off in a different direction. The shadows of darkness, their tentacles wrapping around the land, grew longer, leaving man no choice but to find shelter. Darkness surrounded the dogsled as Johnathan and Shining Star finished their journey to Dawson, reaching Bev's house safely. The barking of the approaching dogs brought the people in Bev's house outside. John, Wendy, and Steward, along with Bev, greeted the couple lovingly. Some news from Bev later in the evening would both shock and intrigue the young couple. With a couple of laughs thrown in, it would be a feel-good story about a donkey who would rather be a mother than work.

CHAPTER SEVENTY-SEVEN

The waiting group of relatives helped unload Johnathan and Shining Star's dogsled. The couple's personal belongings were taken into Bev's house, while the sled and dogs went to their prearranged places. The dog sleds and harness went into the shed while the dogs were tethered to stakes beside the building.

Johnathan and Shining Star visited Honey and Omar before entering the house, where they admired Bev's Christmas tree in the living room, which was decorated with homemade ornaments. Over the years visitors had brought new art they had created to hang on her tree, and it was known as the happiest tree in Dawson. Bev was finishing making dinner. She had decided on cooking a large pot of moose stew with potatoes and carrots, accompanied by fresh baked bread, her specialty. The dinner was filling and flavorful, something the travellers enjoyed. The conversation over dinner was light, until Bev called for quiet. She had something important to tell Johnathan and Shining Star. Honey was pregnant and Omar was the father. There would be no more heavy lifting for Honey until after her baby was born.

Johnathan and Shining Star were surprised, but not

unhappy, by this news. After hearing about the incident on the trail, the couple said this must have been the result of Omar's uncontrolled sex drive. Spontaneous laughter rang out around the table at this comment by the young couple. Johnathan suggested to Shining Star that for a small fee they could have the farrier come and check the status of Honey's pregnancy. Shining Star said no to Johnathan's suggestion, saying the divine spirits would help Honey with her baby and it would be born healthy.

Tomorrow night was Christmas Eve. The tired couple who had travelled all day were exhausted and ready for bed. They said goodnight to their hostess and company and retired upstairs to the bedroom. Johnathan looked out the bedroom window into the darkness. Beyond the trees, the city of Dawson was dark and lifeless; the people were inside their homes trying to keep warm. Large Christmas celebrations were out of reach for most of these desperate people who were trying to stay alive in a land which gave few favors, only death for the unprepared.

The strong aroma of pork frying on the woodstove greeted the senses of Johnathan and Shining Star upon wakening in the morning. A brief time later, Bev called everyone down for breakfast. The smell of fresh baked bread overwhelmed the couple's senses when they entered the kitchen. Soon, the rest of the guests were up and sitting around the kitchen table eating fried pork and bread, fresh out of Bev's oven. The group would spend the day at her house and would be joined by other friends and relatives for dinner and conversation for Christmas Eve. Bev had planned this party so everyone could enjoy the spirit of Christmas.

CHAPTER SEVENTY-EIGHT

The day was bitter cold, the temperature in Dawson would only rise to -20 on the Fahrenheit scale. The nighttime low would be much colder, making it a bitter night indeed, even for Dawson. Regardless of how cold it was outside; Bev's home was a bastion of warmth. The spirit of Christmas and the love it exuded filled Bev's home with a feeling of joy.

After breakfast, Johnathan and Shining Star went to take care of Ginger and Shirley, their two sled dogs. Chase, being the family pet, got to stay inside the house at night, where it was warm, with his two owners. After feeding their dogs and giving them fresh water, the couple went to the barn to visit Omar and Honey. The donkeys' accommodations were beside each other, allowing the two donkeys to rub their heads and necks together when they felt they wanted to cuddle. This pair of donkeys were in love and Honey was expecting Omar's baby. Omar and Honey enjoyed the attention Johnathan and Shining Star lavished on them. Shining Star pointed out a slight bulge in Honey's stomach, saying Honey was showing her pregnancy. Shining Star wasn't sure when Honey's baby would be born but figured it would be sometime next fall. After a lengthy visit with the animals, the couple returned to the house.

Bev was busy preparing for dinner; her menu offered several choices. Moose, venison, and bear roasts were cooking in the oven of the wood stove and turnips, potatoes and carrots were beginning to boil on the burners. These meats and vegetables would be accompanied by fresh baked bread, topped with homemade butter. Bev had saved some fresh apples in her root cellar and had baked two apple pies for dessert, to top off what she hoped was a delicious meal.

Wendy was helping Bev with all the work which needed to be done before Christmas Eve dinner, while Shining Star helped watch Kuzih, Wendy's son. Bev had switched the day of her annual celebration from Christmas Day to Christmas Eve, due to a conflict in the schedule of some of her invited guests. Two elders from her tribe, who had been friends with Bev for too many years to count, had never missed Bev's Christmas dinner in twenty years. However, they were each expected at their children's homes on Christmas Day. Two other relatives of Bev's were also supposed to attend the celebration.

The day passed quickly and soon darkness fell over the Yukon. The cold north wind blew outside, swirling the snow around Bev's home. Her last guests had arrived, and the dinner table was ready, so everyone was seated. Dinner was loud as the guests shared stories amongst themselves. Laughter filled the house as the diners happily ate their meal. The group finished with the apple pie, which everyone enjoyed immensely. The women helped Bev clean up the after-dinner mess, while the men went outside and checked on their dogs. Upon their return, the men retired to the living room to share conversation and admire Bev's Christmas tree, along with the rest of the family and friends. Shining Star hung an ornament she had made on Bev's Christmas tree, which represented the forever love she and Johnathan shared together.

Steward and Jason took the two elders to their respective homes shortly after nine, with everyone else staying at Bev's overnight, sleeping where it was safe and warm. Johnathan and Shining Star would share the floor of their bedroom with John, Wendy, and Kuzih tonight. As everyone retired, Bev's home was full of love, which was sorely needed to survive in this land so far north. Johnathan and Shining Star drifted off to sleep feeling blessed to have found each other and to share a love which they believed would never die.

CHAPTER SEVENTY-NINE

Bev's house sat on the edge of town and was one of the largest and better constructed houses in Dawson. There were three bedrooms, a kitchen that could seat ten, and a large living room and parlour area. A woodshed and outhouse were attached to the house and accessible from inside of the building. Her husband had built a smaller building to process furs and to butcher large game animals such as moose and deer. A large barn had been built by a nephew to accommodate livestock, which was now largely used to board pack animals.

Bev provided much support and community service to the local Indigenous people living around or in Dawson. She was still an active member of the tribe and held a seat high on its council. Her home was used as a staging area for many important events concerning the tribe. The three large outdoor freezers on Bev's property were for any tribal members to use if they needed a place to store their meat. A small donation of meat for this service was appreciated. The donors' gifts would feed the hungriest and most food deprived people in Dawson.

Bev was up at daybreak working in her kitchen,

preparing Christmas breakfast for her guests. Fried pork, potatoes, carrots left over from the previous night's dinner, and fresh baked bread were on the menu. After setting the table and cooking the food, she called everyone to come to the kitchen and eat breakfast. Her guests came downstairs one by one, rubbing the sleep out of their eyes, seating themselves at the kitchen table. When all the guests were in attendance Bev had an announcement to make.

Bev revealed Steward had asked her to share some wonderful news; he had met a woman from his tribe and would be getting married next summer. His new wife would join him to live at his cabin after the ceremony. Everyone at the table, except for Kuzih, stared at Bev in a state of disbelief. When the news sunk in, they congratulated Steward, asking him numerous questions as they ate their breakfast. They were genuinely happy he had found someone to take as a wife, both for companionship and love. Wendy was proud of her brother and wished him all the best for his and his new wife's future.

After breakfast, Bev's invited dinner company left, as they too had family to visit today. With just her family left, the remaining group gathered in the living room to exchange presents. Bev was given the tanned deer skin Shining Star had worked so hard to make for her. Bev gave each of her nieces and her nephew a gift basket filled with difficult to find items while living in the bush. Coffee, sugar, salt, and flour were just a few of the items she included. Shining Star gave Johnathan his beaver skin hat. He had watched her meticulously work on getting the hat perfect for him and loved her gift. He would wear it while working his trapline and on the return trip home.

Johnathan's Christmas gift to Shining Star was special. He had taken one of the gold nuggets they found panning and given it to Wendy, who was a skilled artisan when making jewellery. The nugget now hung on a silver chain crafted by Wendy. Shining Star would wear it on special occasions, like Christmas, otherwise, it would put away for safekeeping.

The day was tiring, but Bev was pleased with how her Christmas gathering had turned out. Tomorrow she would be left alone, as her extended family would return to their cabins and traplines, taking with them memories of a wonderful Christmas celebration and hopes this tradition would happen again for many years to come.

CHAPTER EIGHTY

It was the day after Christmas and Bev's company was getting ready to leave. The two young couples and Steward had been up since sunrise preparing for their journey home. Their sleds were loaded, and the dog teams were ready to go. With a fond farewell to Bev, the group left Dawson. They travelled together at first, eventually parting ways. The dogsleds veered off in different directions to reach their respective destinations, but the occupants knew they would see each other soon. While at Bev's, Johnathan had talked with Jason and Steward about participating in a moose hunt. The men had arranged a date in January to meet at Johnathan and Shining Star's cabin to carry out this venture.

The day was cold and clear. The bright sun shining down on Johnathan and Shining Star provided little warmth. The forest was silent except for the heavy panting of dogs as they pulled the sled and its occupants through the forest. The dogs' forward motion slowed as it became apparent to the animals a wolf pack was defiantly blocking their way. Johnathan brought the dogsled to a stop while he contemplated how to deal with this issue.

While in Dawson, Johnathan learned wolf pelts were in vogue and prices for their coats had skyrocketed. He decided to slowly draw closer to the wolves, shooting one of them and taking its body back to his cabin to be processed for its soft coat. The rebellious reputation of wolves is what had helped make its fur desirable in Europe, thus increasing its value.

Johnathan exited the sled with his rifle in hand. The wolves did not change their positions. Two of these animals were laying in the snow blocking the trail, the wolves oblivious as to what Johnathan was planning to do next. He raised his rifle and took aim at one of these predators. The wolves still did not move. Suddenly, a sound like thunder reverberated throughout the forest. Except for one animal, the wolves bolted off into the safety of the trees. A lone wolf lay dead in the blood-soaked snow, a bullet from Johnathan's rifle lodged in its head.

Shining Star drove the dog team to his location and Johnathan loaded the dead body of the canine on the sled. They continued their journey home, with the dogs making good time. The huskies were energetic and enthused to be heading home, even though it was hard to ignore the smell of the dead wolf riding on the sled.

Shortly after three in the afternoon, the cabin came into view. Roscoe came out of his den to meet the homeowners, hoping they had food to feed him. He had not eaten anything but a squirrel and a couple of mice since the couple left to go to Dawson. Johnathan stopped the dogsled in front of his cabin door. He removed the boards he had placed on the cabin for extra security before leaving for Dawson.

Shining Star entered the cabin to start a fire. The outside air temperature was twenty below zero and a warm cabin would be a godsend after riding on the dogsled all day.

Johnathan put Ginger and Shirley in their enclosure and the body of the wolf in the processing shed. He had already unloaded the couple's personal gear and now stored the sled and other supplies in their prospective places. With his work done and Chase by his side, Johnathan joined his wife in a warming cabin, glad to be home.

CHAPTER EIGHTY-ONE

The darkness of night comes early in the north during December. The lack of sunlight and human contact causes a madness to creep over some of the unfortunate souls living in the Yukon during this time of year. The bitter cold keeps the hardiest individuals confined to their cabins for long periods of time. The stillness of the land and the silence which accompanies it can cause the human mind to go insane. This has resulted in the deaths of many fine men and their dogs, who were afflicted by this curse.

Before going to the fur shed to process the wolf hide, Shining Star and Johnathan enjoyed a cup of coffee together. The aroma of this unique beverage filled the air with a feeling of comfort and relaxation. For Johnathan, it made his mind return to easier times, of when he was raised in an environment where coffee was popular. He would lay in his bed in the morning, the smell of brewing coffee drifting into his room. This moment recaptured that memory which had been lost in Johnathan's mind for years.

Finished working in the shed, Shining Star began to cook dinner and prepare the dogs' meal. Tomorrow the couple would fish the lake, in the hopes of replenishing their personal supply of food as well as providing food for the huskies. The heads and innards of the fish would be saved to use as bait on the trapline. The dogs were fed first, and then Johnathan and Shining Star sat down to eat dinner. The venison was their only choice for the meal, which the couple ate in silence, glad to have this food to share.

Tomorrow morning Johnathan and Shining Star would reset twelve of their traps before spending the rest of the day catching fish to restock their empty supply. As the young couple lay in bed the stillness and quiet captured their minds, the curse of cabin fever trying to invade their brains, making their thoughts a jumbled mess. Wrapping up in one another's arms and sharing love for one another were Johnathan and Shining Star's ways of fighting this curse which sometimes enveloped them.

A strong north wind blew snow across the frozen lake. The howl of a lonely wolf calling for his mate was the only sound to break the stillness of the night as the couple slept soundly in their beds. Tomorrow's sunrise was just beyond the horizon.

CHAPTER EIGHTY-TWO

The morning sky dawned bright and clear, but bitter cold. Johnathan took Chase and walked to the enclosure where Ginger and Shirley were housed. He fed his three dogs and then hooked the animals up to the dogsled. He retrieved the traps and bait from the fur shed and loaded them onto the sled. He returned to the cabin telling Shining Star he was ready to go set the traps.

Shining Star climbed aboard the dogsled, making herself as comfortable as possible. Johnathan signalled his dogs to go and with a burst of adrenalin, the huskies bolted forward. The dogsled made its way down the snow packed trail. The forest was quiet at first, only the heavy panting of the dogs could be heard. As the sled moved further away from the cabin, a loud chorus of ravens could be heard. These scavengers were enjoying the leftovers from a kill a predator had made. Curious, Johnathan changed the sled's direction, leaving the main trail and following the ravens' calls to the kill site. He found the carcass of a deer, which had been killed and eaten by wolves. The ravens were eating small morsels of meat dropped by the pack of wolves during their feast on this unfortunate animal.

Johnathan left this scene of nature and turned the dogsled back in the direction of the trail. Over the next two hours he and Shining Star set their twelve traps. There were many rabbits in the area, their tracks visible everywhere. Shining Star suggested they set snares out, and like the fur bearing traps, they would check them daily. This would increase their overall food supply and provide much needed meat for the dogs.

The couple set six snares, hoping to catch the rabbits who wandered the forest unhindered, except for trying to avoid an occasional hungry fox. It seemed the foxes were always left floundering in the snow, while the rabbits escaped on their hard packed runways which meandered through the forest. The rabbit snare was an ingenious invention, a thin wire tied to a sturdy branch hanging low over the rabbits' runway. A loop made in the wire, large enough to snare the rabbit's neck, was placed directly in the runway. An unsuspecting rabbit, hopping along the bunny trail, would catch his neck in this loop, strangling him quickly, thus not making the animal suffer. Trappers often relied on these rabbits for survival, as sometimes it was the only meat available. Many trappers lives were saved by this sometimes-abundant mammal native to these northern forests.

The couple headed back to their cabin as soon as they were done setting the traps and snares. They ate lunch and warmed their weary bones by a roaring fire before going fishing. Johnathan grabbed an axe to reopen the hole in the ice, which had frozen over while they were in Dawson. A large opening in the ice was needed for Shining Star to use her fishing net.

Reaching the area where the old hole had been located, Johnathan spent thirty minutes creating an opening for the fishing net. Shining Star successfully harvested eight whitefish and two lake trout, all of which were of a larger than average size. The couple returned to the cabin, cold but happy, with an abundant supply of meat to feed the family.

CHAPTER EIGHTY-THREE

Over the next two weeks, the couple had twenty-four traps on their line, rabbit snares, and a few beaver traps set by the dam. They worked on checking their traps and rabbit snares daily, with a sizable amount of fur being harvested. Most of the animals caught in the traps were small mammals, but a few larger animals, such as a fox, a bobcat, and two beavers, were harvested as well.

The planned date for the moose hunt with Jason and Steward had arrived. The two men would be arriving at Johnathan and Shining Star's cabin today. Johnathan had checked the marsh where he had seen moose sign before Christmas; the signs suggested this large animal was still living in the area. Jason and Steward arrived at Johnathan and Shining Star's cabin after lunch. They were quite pleased when Johnathan shared the moose was still in the area. It had not moved from the original location where he had seen the initial signs of this large game animal. The trio of men decided to leave at sunrise tomorrow to hunt the moose.

This afternoon the men used two dogsleds to go look at Johnathan's trapline and the emergency shelters. Johnathan showed Jason and Steward the area where the moose was living. They found some tracks in the snow, which Steward identified as being those of a large male moose. The men were hoping for success, which would provide enough meat to fill the outdoor freezers of all three men if they killed and harvested the meat from a large bull moose. The men turned the sleds around and the dogs, with much exuberance, bounded back toward Johnathan's cabin.

The day was sunny and cold, the white snow sparkling in the sunshine made the landscape a wonderland in the eyes of the mushers. The men and the dogsleds arrived without incident back at Johnathan's cabin, where Shining Star was cooking a large pot of beaver stew for dinner. This stew was a favorite of all three of these wilderness trappers. The men took care of their dogs and then went inside. The strong aroma of beaver stew cooking on the woodstove filled their senses, making the stomachs of all three men yearn for this food even more.

The men relaxed and snoozed while Shining Star finished preparing dinner. She roused the men, telling them the food would be ready after they took care of feeding their dogs. Bev had put frozen vegetables in Shining Star's Christmas hamper, as well as a small bag of herbs she had collected and dried. There were enough vegetables for one stew, and the seasonings made it extra tasty. Everyone in the party, including Chase, were soon seated and eating the delicious stew courtesy of the wilderness trappers, Johnathan and Shining Star. This dinner led to a good night's sleep, with the men dreaming of tomorrow's adventure, the hunt for the bull moose.

CHAPTER EIGHTY-FOUR

The morning sky was cloudy with a few snow flurries. Shining Star had risen before the sun was up over the horizon and was preparing breakfast for the men who were going hunting this morning. Fish from the lake and fresh fry bread were on the menu. The items in Bev's hamper, such as the flour and salt, were a special gift these isolated people rarely saw. Making bread was a luxury when living in the wilds of the Yukon. The men were soon up and ready to eat. Wasting no time, they quickly ate, thanking Shining Star as they headed out the door with visions of bull moose in their heads.

The men decided to take two dog teams on the hunt. If they shot a moose, one of the men would return to tell Shining Star. She would take the third dog team to the kill scene, where she would help with the butchering and transporting of the meat. The dogs were fed first, followed by a lot of drama as the animals were connected to their rightful sleds. The trio of moose hunters left the cabin and traveled to the last emergency shelter on Johnathan's trapline. Here they secured their dog teams as they headed into the marsh.

The men walked toward the area where they believed the moose was living, with Johnathan leading the way. Moose sign increased as they moved closer to the site. Johnathan stopped the men when they entered an open area surrounded by woods. He suggested they take cover amongst the trees and watch the treeline, as he was sure this was where the moose was hiding.

Two hours passed with the men quietly watching and waiting for their prey to make an appearance. Steward nudged his hunting companions, as a large rack of antlers appeared first out of the trees. The massive body of a bull moose followed behind. The men held their fire until the animal had cleared the woods. Simultaneously three gunshots rang out, the noise echoing through the forest. A sudden silence prevailed as the men watched the moose stumble backwards, all three bullets having met their mark. He fell dead in the snow, one of the bullets finding the animal's heart.

Adrenalin raced through the bodies of these men as they walked to claim their prize. With this one animal, Mother Nature had provided meat for three cabins until the spring arrived. Jason and Steward stayed with the moose while Johnathan went back to the cabin to tell Shining Star of their success. Gathering up additional tools for butchering this large animal, he returned to the kill site. Shining Star followed shortly after with the other dogsled. She knew killing the moose was the easy part of the job; butchering this large animal and safely storing the meat would be an all-day commitment. However, she knew it was a job which had to be undertaken to help ensure the couple's survival.

CHAPTER EIGHTY-FIVE

Upon his return to the shelter, Johnathan noticed the other dog team was gone. He assumed Jason and Steward had come and taken the dogsled to the kill site. He turned his sled and followed their trail to where the moose lay dead. The men had brought implements of their own to butcher the moose; experience and sharp tools make for a good butcher. Jason and Steward possessed both advantages. Johnathan watched as Jason and Steward skillfully butchered the large animal.

Loud barking caught the men's attention; Shining Star had arrived with her dogsled. She pulled in close to where Jason and Steward were butchering the moose. She laughed at Johnathan, who was standing back watching the men work. She asked Johnathan if he was learning anything and he assured her he learned a lot by watching such skilled hands at work.

Johnathan piled the first load of the meat on Shining Star's sled. All the meat from the carcass of the moose would be taken to Johnathan's cabin. Once there it would be further processed and divided up equally between the three men who participated in the hunt. Johnathan was the rightful owner of the large rack of antlers which would hang proudly from the front of his cabin. They would serve as a testament to Johnathan's abilities as a hunter and provider in this savage land called the Yukon.

By early afternoon, the men had completed butchering the moose. The unusable parts of the animal were left for the scavengers to pick over. Steward's dogsled was the last to leave the remains, as he gathered extra scraps to feed his dogs and bait his traps. At times it seemed he never had enough of these two necessities which would help him in his fight to survive in this cruel land in Canada's north.

When Steward arrived back at Johnathan's cabin, the trio were in the shed cutting the moose into more manageable sizes. Johnathan and Shining Star's share was cut and packaged into small servings and stored in their outdoor freezer. The meat Steward and Jason would take home to their prospective cabins tomorrow were left in large pieces and locked up in the shed overnight. The wolf pack and other predators would be more interested in the remains the men had left in the bush than looking near the cabin.

The job completed; the group returned to the cabin with moose steaks in hand. Shining Star would cook the meat for dinner, while the dogs would be rewarded handsomely for the patience they showed while the men butchered the moose. Large helpings of the trimmings from the moose were dished out to the hungry dogs, who had waited all day for this meal. The same was said for the humans, who like the dogs, gorged on the fresh moose meat, a delicacy in the bush men rarely enjoyed.

CHAPTER EIGHTY-SIX

Early the following morning Jason and Steward loaded their moose meat onto their sleds and headed home to their cabins. Jason's wife Wendy would be both happy and surprised at the good luck the men had on their hunt. She missed Jason dearly and prayed for his safe return home.

The day was bright and sunny as Jason and Steward left Johnathan and Shining Star's cabin on their dogsleds. The snow thrown from the sleds' runners created a cloud of white as the dogs and men disappeared from the couple's view. A veil of silence fell over the land, as Johnathan and Shining Star returned to their cabin to plan their day.

The couple needed to check their trapline, which had been ignored for a couple of days. In completing this task, an unpleasant surprise awaited them. Chase felt lazy today and did not want to pull the sled or even go outside in the cold. He was just not in the mood for working. He thought about feigning sickness but knew in his heart it was important to Johnathan to get this work done and he could not let his best friend down. Chase made the right choice by helping, instead of hindering Johnathan.

Johnathan readied the dogs, attaching their harnesses

to the sled. He mushed the animals over to the cabin, where Shining Star was waiting to be picked up. The bright sunshine raised the spirits of both man and dogs as the sled raced down the trail. The first six traps Shining Star and Johnathan checked held no fur. The following trap led to an unfortunate, but familiar, incident; a half-eaten animal was in the trap, its fur littering the surrounding snow.

The couple knew who the culprit was, as wolverine tracks were plentiful in the area. Another one of their biggest foes had duped them again. Their feelings went from happy to sullen, knowing they had to deal with one of these destructive animals again. The rest of the trapline produced good results, six fur bearing mammals were caught and taken back to the cabin. Their hides would be added to the ones already stored in the shed.

The days of January moved quickly into the month of February. The couple were now losing one or two animals a day to the wolverine. He had made the trapline his personal feeding station. The wolverine had eluded the traps Johnathan and Shining Star had set for him and was now even harassing them at their cabin. It was a battle of wits between man and beast, with no clear winner.

EPILOGUE

The lure of the Yukon and its wilderness tempted Johnathan and Shining Star to choose a life few would want, an existence in a harsh land where only the strongest survive. The month of February saw the wolverine disappear. Tired of owning this territory, the animal moved on to discover another.

As spring drew closer, Johnathan knew the trapping season would soon end. Before the snow melted, they took their furs to Dawson to be sold. In April the landscape changed, the snow melted, and life returned to the Yukon.

The big news for the young couple was that Shining Star was pregnant. She was expected to have her baby in the fall. The couple decided if the baby was born healthy, they would spend the winter in Dawson. Shining Star's aunt, Bev, would help ensure the survival of her new baby through its first Yukon winter. Honey and her new baby would be gifted to Bev. She could use Honey as a pack animal when needed by her tribe.

The story of Johnathan and Shining Star's life in the

wilderness is a tale which could not be repeated today. The love and commitment by these young lovers helped assure their survival in the early settlement of the Yukon, a land better known as God's country, a land which time forgot.

ACKNOWLEDGEMENTS

I would like to extend my thanks to my wife, Ruth Ann, who assisted in editing this work. Without her patience and understanding, publishing this book would have been more difficult. The task was made easier by a devoted woman who worked diligently to finish this project.